ESSENTIAL POEMS

SIGNATURE EDITIONS

ESSENTIAL POEMS

EMILY DICKINSON

UNION SQUARE & CO.
NEW YORK

UNION
SQUARE
& CO.

NEW YORK

UNION SQUARE & CO. and the distinctive Union Square & Co. logo are trademarks of Sterling Publishing Co., Inc.

Union Square & Co., LLC, is a subsidiary of Sterling Publishing Co., Inc.

This 2025 edition published by Union Square & Co., LLC

A Note on the Text: This collection was originally published in 1924 and reflects the attitudes of its time. The publisher's decision to present it as it was first published is not intended as endorsement of any offensive cultural representations or language.

ISBN 978-1-4549-6084-3
ISBN 978-1-4549-6085-0 (e-book)

For information about custom editions, special sales, and premium purchases, please contact specialsales@unionsquareandco.com.

Printed in India

REP

2 4 6 8 10 9 7 5 3

unionsquareandco.com

Cover design by Igor Satanovsky and David Ter-Avanesyan
Cover images: Shutterstock.com: AlbertLin123/(flowers), ismail19797 (bird); courtesy of Wikimedia Commons (writing)

CONTENTS

INTRODUCTION

THE POEMS OF EMILY DICKINSON, PUBLISHED IN A SERIES OF three volumes at various intervals after her death in 1886, and in a volume entitled "The Single Hound," published in 1914, with the addition of a few before omitted, are here collected in a final complete edition.

In them and in her "Life and Letters," recently presented in one inclusive volume, lives all of Emily Dickinson—for the outward circumstance matters little, nor is this the place for discussion as to whether fate ordained her or she ordained her own foreordination.

Many of her poems have been reprinted in anthologies, selections, textbooks for recitation, and they have increasingly found their elect and been best interpreted by the expansion of those lives they have seized upon by force of their natural, profound intuition of the miracles of everyday Life, Love, and Death.

She herself was of the part of life that is always youth, always magical. She wrote of it as she grew to know it, step by step, discovery by discovery, truth by truth—until time merely became eternity. She was preeminently the discoverer—eagerly hunting the meaning of it all; this strange world in which she wonderingly found herself,—"A Balboa of house and garden," surmising what lay beyond the purple horizon. She lived with a God we do not believe in, and trusted in an immortality we do not deserve, in that confiding age when Duty ruled over Pleasure before the Puritan became a hypocrite.

Her aspect of Deity,—as her intimation,—was her own,—unique, peculiar, unimpaired by the brimstone theology of her day.

Her poems reflect this direct relation toward the great realities we have later avoided, covered up, or tried to wipe out; perhaps because were they really so great we become so small in consequence. All truth came to Emily straight from honor to honor unimpaired. She never trafficked with falsehood seriously, never employed a deception in thought or feeling of her own. This pitiless sincerity dictated:

> I like a look of agony
> Because I know it's true
> Men do not sham convulsion
> Nor simulate a throe.

As light after darkness, Summer following Winter, she is inevitable, unequivocal. Evasion of fact she knew not, though her body might flit away from interruption, leaving an intruder to "Think that a sunbeam left the door ajar."

Her entities were vast—as her words were few; those words like dry-point etching or frost upon the pane! Doubly aspected, every event, every object seemed to hold for her both its actual and imaginative dimension. By this power she carries her readers behind the veil obscuring less gifted apprehension. She even descends over the brink of the grave to toy with the outworn vesture of the spirit, recapture the dead smile on lips surrendered forever; then, as on the wings of Death, betakes herself and her reader in the direction of the escaping soul to new, incredible heights.

Doubly her life carried on, two worlds in her brown eyes, by which habit of the Unseen she confessed:

> I fit for them,
> I seek the dark till I am thorough fit.

The labor is a solemn one,
With this sufficient sweet—
That abstinence as mine produce
A purer good for them,
If I succeed,—
If not, I had
The transport of the Aim.

This transport of the aim absorbed her, and this absorption is her clearest explanation,—the absorption in This excluding observance of That. Most of all she was busy. It takes time even for genius to crystallize the thought with which her letters and poems are crammed. Her solitude was never idle.

Her awe of that unknown sacrament of love permeated all she wrote, and before Nature, God, and Death she is more fearless than that archangel of portentous shadow she instinctively dreaded.

Almost transfigured by reverence, her poems are pervaded by inference sharply in contrast to the balder speech of to-day. Here the mystic suppressed the woman, though her heart leaped up over children,—radiant phenomena to her, akin to stars fallen among her daffodils in the orchard; and her own renunciation, chalice at lip, was nobly, frankly given in the poem ending:

Each bound the other's crucifix,
We gave no other bond.
Sufficient troth that we shall rise—
Deposed, at length, the grave—
To that new marriage, justified
Through Calvaries of Love!

Her own philosophy had early taught her that All was in All: there were no degrees in anything. Accordingly nothing was mean or trivial, and her "fainting robin" became a synonym of the universe. She saw in absolute terms which gave her poetry an accuracy like that obtained under the microscope of modern science. But her soul dominated, and when her footsteps wavered her terms were still dictated by her unquenchable spirit.

Hers too were spirit terms with life and friends, in which respect she was of a divergence from the usual not easily to be condoned.

It was precisely the clamor of the commonplace exasperated by the austerities of a reserved individuality, that provoked her immortal exclamation:

> Much madness is divinest sense
> To a discerning eye.
> Much sense the starkest madness;
> 'T is the majority
> In this, as all prevails.
> Assent and you are sane—
> Demur—you're straightaway dangerous
> And handled with a chain.

Her interpretation demands height and depth of application in her readers, for although her range is that of any soul not earth-bound by the senses, she does not always make it immediately plain when she speaks out of her own vision in her own tongue. In spite of which, beyond those who profess her almost as a cult, she is supremely the poet of those who "never read poetry." The scoffers, the literary agnostics, make exception for her. She is also the poet of the unpoetic, the unlearned foreigner, the busy, practical, inexpressive man as well as woman, the wise young and groping old, the nature worshipper, the schoolgirl, children caught by her fairy lineage, and lovers of all degree.

Full many a preacher has found her line at the heart of his matter and left her verse to fly up with his conclusion. And it is the Very Reverend head of a most Catholic order who writes, "I bless God for Emily,—some of her writings have had a more profound influence on my life than anything else that any one has ever written."

Mystic to mystic, mind to mind, spirit to spirit, dust to dust. She was at the source of things and dwelt beside the very springs of life, yet those deep wells from which she drew were of the wayside, though their waters were of eternal truth, her magnificat one of the certainties of every immortal being. Here in her poems the arisen Emily, unabashed by mortal bonds, speaks to her "Divine Majority":

> Split the lark and you'll find the music—
> Bulb after bulb, in silver rolled,
> Scantily dealt to the Summer morning,
> Saved for your ears when lutes are old.

But in what vernacular explain the skylark to the mole—even she was at loss to tell. And for the true lovers of the prose or poetry of Emily Dickinson, explanation of her is as impertinent as unnecessary.

MARTHA DICKINSON BIANCHI.
Siena,
March, 1924.

NOTE

For the convenience of readers familiar with previous editions of Emily Dickinson's poems the original four divisions have here been retained, each now including all the poems of its own group in the three volumes of the series.

The names given to many of the poems by former editors have been dropped, leaving them as they were found in manuscript,—not entitled; but the old landmarks of "Life, Nature, Love, Time and Eternity" remain at suggestion of the publisher, for whose kind consideration I make sincere acknowledgment, as also for the invaluable assistance of Alfred Leete Hampson.

M. D. B.

PART ONE

Life

This is my letter to the world,
That never wrote to me,—
The simple news that Nature told,
With tender majesty.

Her message is committed
To hands I cannot see;
For love of her, sweet countrymen,
Judge tenderly of me!

I

Success is counted sweetest
By those who ne'er succeed.
To comprehend a nectar
Requires sorest need.

Not one of all the purple host
Who took the flag to-day
Can tell the definition,
So clear, of victory,

As he, defeated, dying,
On whose forbidden ear
The distant strains of triumph
Break, agonized and clear.

II

Our share of night to bear,
Our share of morning,
Our blank in bliss to fill.
Our blank in scorning.

Here a star, and there a star,
Some lose their way.
Here a mist, and there a mist,
Afterwards—day!

III

Soul, wilt thou toss again?
By just such a hazard
Hundreds have lost, indeed,
But tens have won an all.

Angels' breathless ballot
Lingers to record thee;
Imps in eager caucus
Raffle for my soul.

IV

'T is so much joy! 'T is so much joy!
If I should fail, what poverty!
And yet, as poor as I
Have ventured all upon a throw;
Have gained! Yes! Hesitated so
This side the victory!

Life is but life, and death but death!
Bliss is but bliss, and breath but breath!
And if, indeed, I fail,
At least to know the worst is sweet.
Defeat means nothing but defeat,
No drearier can prevail!

And if I gain,—oh, gun at sea,
Oh, bells that in the steeples be,
At first repeat it slow!
For heaven is a different thing
Conjectured, and waked sudden in,
And might o'erwhelm me so!

V

Glee! the great storm is over!
Four have recovered the land;
Forty gone down together
Into the boiling sand.

Ring, for the scant salvation!
Toll, for the bonnie souls,—
Neighbor and friend and bridegroom,
Spinning upon the shoals!

How they will tell the shipwreck
When winter shakes the door,
Till the children ask, "But the forty?
Did they come back no more?"
Then a silence suffuses the story,

And a softness the teller's eye;
And the children no further question,
And only the waves reply.

VI

If I can stop one heart from breaking,
I shall not live in vain;
If I can ease one life the aching,
Or cool one pain,
Or help one fainting robin
Unto his nest again,
I shall not live in vain.

VII

Within my reach!
I could have touched!
I might have chanced that way!
Soft sauntered through the village,
Sauntered as soft away!
So unsuspected violets
Within the fields lie low,
Too late for striving fingers
That passed, an hour ago.

VIII

A wounded deer leaps highest,
I've heard the hunter tell;
'T is but the ecstasy of death,
And then the brake is still.

The smitten rock that gushes,
The trampled steel that springs:
A cheek is always redder
Just where the hectic stings!

Mirth is the mail of anguish,
In which it caution arm,
Lest anybody spy the blood
And "You're hurt" exclaim!

IX

The heart asks pleasure first,
And then, excuse from pain;
And then, those little anodynes
That deaden suffering;

And then, to go to sleep;
And then, if it should be
The will of its Inquisitor,
The liberty to die.

X

A precious, mouldering pleasure 't is
To meet an antique book,
In just the dress his century wore;
A privilege, I think,

His venerable hand to take,
And warming in our own,
A passage back, or two, to make
To times when he was young.

His quaint opinions to inspect,
His knowledge to unfold
On what concerns our mutual mind,
The literature of old;

What interested scholars most,
What competitions ran
When Plato was a certainty,
And Sophocles a man;

When Sappho was a living girl,
And Beatrice wore
The gown that Dante deified.
Facts, centuries before,

He traverses familiar,
As one should come to town
And tell you all your dreams were true:
He lived where dreams were born.

His presence is enchantment,
You beg him not to go;
Old volumes shake their vellum heads
And tantalize, just so.

XI

Much madness is divinest sense
To a discerning eye;
Much sense the starkest madness.
'T is the majority
In this, as all, prevails.
Assent, and you are sane;
Demur,—you're straightaway dangerous,
And handled with a chain.

XII

I asked no other thing,
No other was denied.
I offered Being for it;
The mighty merchant smiled.

Brazil? He twirled a button,
Without a glance my way:
"But, madam, is there nothing else
That we can show to-day?"

XIII

The soul selects her own society,
Then shuts the door;
On her divine majority
Obtrude no more.

Unmoved, she notes the chariot's pausing
At her low gate;

Unmoved, an emperor is kneeling
Upon her mat.

I've known her from an ample nation
Choose one;
Then close the valves of her attention
Like stone.

XIV

Some things that fly there be,—
Birds, hours, the bumble-bee:
Of these no elegy.

Some things that stay there be
Grief, hills, eternity:
Nor this behooveth me.

There are, that resting, rise.
Can I expound the skies?
How still the riddle lies!

XV

I know some lonely houses off the road
A robber 'd like the look of,—
Wooden barred,
And windows hanging low,
Inviting to
A portico,

Where two could creep:
One hand the tools,
The other peep
To make sure all's asleep.
Old-fashioned eyes,
Not easy to surprise!

How orderly the kitchen 'd look by night,
With just a clock,—
But they could gag the tick,
And mice won't bark;
And so the walls don't tell,
None will.

A pair of spectacles ajar just stir—
An almanac's aware.
Was it the mat winked,
Or a nervous star?
The moon slides down the stair
To see who's there.

There's plunder,—where?
Tankard, or spoon,
Earring, or stone,
A watch, some ancient brooch
To match the grandmamma,
Staid sleeping there.

Day rattles, too,
Stealth's slow;
The sun has got as far
As the third sycamore.
Screams chanticleer,
"Who's there?"

And echoes, trains away,
Sneer—"Where?"
While the old couple, just astir,
Think that the sunrise left the door ajar!

XVI

To fight aloud is very brave,
But gallanter, I know,

Who charge within the bosom,
The cavalry of woe.

Who win, and nations do not see,
Who fall, and none observe,
Whose dying eyes no country
Regards with patriot love.

We trust, in plumed procession,
For such the angels go,
Rank after rank, with even feet
And uniforms of snow.

XVII

When night is almost done,
And sunrise grows so near
That we can touch the spaces,
It's time to smooth the hair

And get the dimples ready,
And wonder we could care
For that old faded midnight
That frightened but an hour.

XVIII

Read, sweet, how others strove,
Till we are stouter;
What they renounced,
Till we are less afraid;
How many times they bore
The faithful witness,
Till we are helped,
As if a kingdom cared!

Read then of faith
That shone above the fagot;
Clear strains of hymn
The river could not drown;
Brave names of men
And celestial women,
Passed out of record
Into renown!

XIX

Pain has an element of blank;
It cannot recollect
When it began, or if there were
A day when it was not.

It has no future but itself,
Its infinite realms contain
Its past, enlightened to perceive
New periods of pain.

XX

I taste a liquor never brewed,
From tankards scooped in pearl;
Not all the vats upon the Rhine
Yield such an alcohol!

Inebriate of air am I,
And debauchee of dew,
Reeling, through endless summer days,
From inns of molten blue.

When landlords turn the drunken bee
Out of the foxglove's door,
When butterflies renounce their drams,
I shall but drink the more!

Till seraphs swing their snowy hats,
And saints to windows run,
To see the little tippler
Leaning against the sun!

XXI

He ate and drank the precious words,
His spirit grew robust;
He knew no more that he was poor,
Nor that his frame was dust.
He danced along the dingy days,
And this bequest of wings
Was but a book. What liberty
A loosened spirit brings!

XXII

I had no time to hate, because
The grave would hinder me,
And life was not so ample I
Could finish enmity.

Nor had I time to love; but since
Some industry must be,
The little toil of love, I thought,
Was large enough for me.

XXIII

'T was such a little, little boat
That toddled down the bay!
'T was such a gallant, gallant sea
That beckoned it away!

'T was such a greedy, greedy wave
That licked it from the coast;

Nor ever guessed the stately sails
My little craft was lost!

XXIV

Whether my bark went down at sea,
Whether she met with gales,
Whether to isles enchanted
She bent her docile sails;

By what mystic mooring
She is held to-day,—
This is the errand of the eye
Out upon the bay.

XXV

Belshazzar had a letter,—
He never had but one;
Belshazzar's correspondent
Concluded and begun
In that immortal copy
The conscience of us all
Can read without its glasses
On revelation's wall.

XXVI

The brain within its groove
Runs evenly and true;
But let a splinter swerve,
'T were easier for you
To put the water back
When floods have slit the hills,
And scooped a turnpike for themselves,
And blotted out the mills!

XXVII

I'm nobody! Who are you?
Are you nobody, too?
Then there's a pair of us—don't tell!
They'd banish us, you know.

How dreary to be somebody!
How public, like a frog
To tell your name the livelong day
To an admiring bog!

XXVIII

I bring an unaccustomed wine
To lips long parching, next to mine,
And summon them to drink.

Crackling with fever, they essay;
I turn my brimming eyes away,
And come next hour to look.

The hands still hug the tardy glass;
The lips I would have cooled, alas!
Are so superfluous cold,

I would as soon attempt to warm
The bosoms where the frost has lain
Ages beneath the mould.

Some other thirsty there may be
To whom this would have pointed me
Had it remained to speak.

And so I always bear the cup
If, haply, mine may be the drop
Some pilgrim thirst to slake,—

If, haply, any say to me,
"Unto the little, unto me,"
When I at last awake.

XXIX

The nearest dream recedes, unrealized.
The heaven we chase
Like the June bee
Before the school-boy
Invites the race;
Stoops to an easy clover—
Dips—evades—teases—deploys;
Then to the royal clouds
Lifts his light pinnace
Heedless of the boy
Staring, bewildered, at the mocking sky.

Homesick for steadfast honey,
Ah! the bee flies not
That brews that rare variety.

XXX

We play at paste,
Till qualified for pearl,
Then drop the paste,
And deem ourself a fool.
The shapes, though, were similar,
And our new hands
Learned gem-tactics
Practising sands.

XXXI

I found the phrase to every thought
I ever had, but one;
And that defies me,—as a hand
Did try to chalk the sun

To races nurtured in the dark;—
How would your own begin?
Can blaze be done in cochineal,
Or noon in mazarin?

XXXII

Hope is the thing with feathers
That perches in the soul,
And sings the tune without the words,
And never stops at all,

And sweetest in the gale is heard;
And sore must be the storm
That could abash the little bird
That kept so many warm.

I've heard it in the chillest land,
And on the strangest sea;
Yet, never, in extremity,
It asked a crumb of me.

XXXIII

Dare you see a soul at the white heat?
  Then crouch within the door.
Red is the fire's common tint;
  But when the vivid ore

Has sated flame's conditions,
  Its quivering substance plays
Without a color but the light
  Of unanointed blaze.

Least village boasts its blacksmith,
  Whose anvil's even din
Stands symbol for the finer forge
  That soundless tugs within,

Refining these impatient ores
  With hammer and with blaze,
Until the designated light
  Repudiate the forge.

XXXIV

Who never lost, are unprepared
A coronet to find;
Who never thirsted, flagons
And cooling tamarind.

Who never climbed the weary league—
Can such a foot explore
The purple territories
On Pizarro's shore?

How many legions overcome?
The emperor will say.
How many colors taken
On Revolution Day?

How many bullets bearest?
The royal scar hast thou?
Angels, write "Promoted"
On this soldier's brow!

XXXV

I can wade grief,
Whole pools of it,—
I'm used to that.
But the least push of joy
Breaks up my feet,
And I tip—drunken.
Let no pebble smile,
'T was the new liquor,—
That was all!

Power is only pain,
Stranded, through discipline,
Till weights will hang.
Give balm to giants,
And they'll wilt, like men.
Give Himmaleh,—
They'll carry him!

XXXVI

I never hear the word "escape"
Without a quicker blood,
A sudden expectation,
A flying attitude.

I never hear of prisons broad
By soldiers battered down,
But I tug childish at my bars,—
Only to fail again!

XXXVII

For each ecstatic instant
We must an anguish pay

In keen and quivering ratio
To the ecstasy.

For each beloved hour
Sharp pittances of years,
Bitter contested farthings
And coffers heaped with tears.

XXXVIII

Through the straight pass of suffering
The martyrs even trod,
Their feet upon temptation,
Their faces upon God.

A stately, shriven company;
Convulsion playing round,
Harmless as streaks of meteor
Upon a planet's bound.

Their faith the everlasting troth;
Their expectation fair;
The needle to the north degree
Wades so, through polar air.

XXXIX

I meant to have but modest needs,
Such as content, and heaven;
Within my income these could lie,
And life and I keep even.

But since the last included both,
It would suffice my prayer
But just for one to stipulate,
And grace would grant the pair.

And so, upon this wise I prayed,—
Great Spirit, give to me
A heaven not so large as yours,
But large enough for me.

A smile suffused Jehovah's face;
The cherubim withdrew;
Grave saints stole out to look at me,
And showed their dimples, too.

I left the place with all my might,—
My prayer away I threw;
The quiet ages picked it up,
And Judgment twinkled, too,

That one so honest be extant
As take the tale for true
That "Whatsoever you shall ask,
Itself be given you."

But I, grown shrewder, scan the skies
With a suspicious air,—
As children, swindled for the first,
All swindlers be, infer.

XL

The thought beneath so slight a film
Is more distinctly seen,—
As laces just reveal the surge,
Or mists the Apennine.

XLI

The soul unto itself
Is an imperial friend,—

Or the most agonizing! spy
An enemy could send.

Secure against its own,
No treason it can fear;
Itself its sovereign, of itself
The soul should stand in awe.

XLII

Surgeons must be very careful
When they take the knife!
Underneath their fine incisions
Stirs the culprit,—Life!

XLIII

I like to see it lap the miles,
And lick the valleys up,
And stop to feed itself at tanks;
And then, prodigious, step

Around a pile of mountains,
And, supercilious, peer
In shanties by the sides of roads;
And then a quarry pare

To fit its sides, and crawl between,
Complaining all the while
In horrid, hooting stanza;
Then chase itself down hill

And neigh like Boanerges;
Then, punctual as a star,
Stop—docile and omnipotent—
At its own stable door.

XLIV

The show is not the show,
But they that go.
Menagerie to me
My neighbor be.
Fair play—
Both went to see.

XLV

Delight becomes pictorial
When viewed through pain,—
More fair, because impossible
That any gain.

The mountain at a given distance
In amber lies;
Approached, the amber flits a little,—
And that's the skies!

XLVI

A thought went up my mind to-day
That I have had before,
But did not finish,—some way back,
I could not fix the year,

Nor where it went, nor why it came
The second time to me,
Nor definitely what it was,
Have I the art to say.

But somewhere in my soul, I know
I've met the thing before;

It just reminded me—'t was all—
And came my way no more.

XLVII

Is Heaven a physician?
They say that He can heal;
But medicine posthumous
Is unavailable.

Is Heaven an exchequer?
They speak of what we owe;
But that negotiation
I'm not a party to.

XLVIII

Though I get home how late, how late!
So I get home, 't will compensate.
Better will be the ecstasy
That they have done expecting me,
When, night descending, dumb and dark,
They hear my unexpected knock.
Transporting must the moment be,
Brewed from decades of agony!

To think just how the fire will burn,
Just how long-cheated eyes will turn
To wonder what myself will say,
And what itself will say to me,
Beguiles the centuries of way!

XLIX

A poor torn heart, a tattered heart,
That sat it down to rest,

Nor noticed that the ebbing day
Flowed silver to the west,
Nor noticed night did soft descend
Nor constellation burn,
Intent upon the vision
Of latitudes unknown.

The angels, happening that way,
This dusty heart espied;
Tenderly took it up from toil
And carried it to God.
There,—sandals for the barefoot;
There,—gathered from the gales,
Do the blue havens by the hand
Lead the wandering sails.

L

I should have been too glad, I see,
Too lifted for the scant degree
  Of life's penurious round;
My little circuit would have shamed
This new circumference, have blamed
  The homelier time behind.

I should have been too saved, I see,
Too rescued; fear too dim to me
  That I could spell the prayer
I knew so perfect yesterday,—
That scalding one, "Sabachthani,"
  Recited fluent here.

Earth would have been too much, I see,
And heaven not enough for me;
  I should have had the joy
Without the fear to justify,—

The palm without the Calvary;
  So, Saviour, crucify.
Defeat whets victory, they say;
The reefs in old Gethsemane
  Endear the shore beyond.
'T is beggars banquets best define;
'T is thirsting vitalizes wine,—
  Faith faints to understand.

LI

It tossed and tossed,—
A little brig I knew,—
O'ertook by blast,
It spun and spun,
And groped delirious, for morn.

It slipped and slipped,
As one that drunken stepped;
Its white foot tripped,
Then dropped from sight.

Ah, brig, good-night
To crew and you;
The ocean's heart too smooth, too blue,
To break for you.

LII

Victory comes late,
And is held low to freezing lips
Too rapt with frost
To take it.

How sweet it would have tasted,
Just a drop!

Was God so economical?
His table's spread too high for us
Unless we dine on tip-toe.
Crumbs fit such little mouths,
Cherries suit robins;
The eagle's golden breakfast
Strangles them.
God keeps his oath to sparrows,
Who of little love
Know how to starve!

LIII

God gave a loaf to every bird,
But just a crumb to me;
I dare not eat it, though I starve,—
My poignant luxury
To own it, touch it, prove the feat
That made the pellet mine,—
Too happy in my sparrow chance
For ampler coveting.

It might be famine all around,
I could not miss an ear,
Such plenty smiles upon my board,
My garner shows so fair.
I wonder how the rich may feel,—
An Indiaman—an Earl?
I deem that I with but a crumb
Am sovereign of them all.

LIV

Experiment to me
Is every one I meet.

If it contain a kernel?
The figure of a nut

Presents upon a tree,
Equally plausibly;
But meat within is requisite,
To squirrels and to me.

LV

My country need not change her gown,
Her triple suit as sweet
As when 't was cut at Lexington,
And first pronounced "a fit."

Great Britain disapproves "the stars";
Disparagement discreet,—
There's something in their attitude
That taunts her bayonet.

LVI

Faith is a fine invention
For gentlemen who see;
But microscopes are prudent
In an emergency!

LVII

Except the heaven had come so near,
So seemed to choose my door,
The distance would not haunt me so;
I had not hoped before.

But just to hear the grace depart
I never thought to see,

Afflicts me with a double loss;
'T is lost, and lost to me.

LVIII

Portraits are to daily faces
As an evening west
To a fine, pedantic sunshine
In a satin vest.

LIX

I took my power in my hand
And went against the world;
'T was not so much as David had,
But I was twice as bold.

I aimed my pebble, but myself
Was all the one that fell.
Was it Goliath was too large,
Or only I too small?

LX

A shady friend for torrid days
Is easier to find
Than one of higher temperature
For frigid hour of mind.

The vane a little to the east
Scares muslin souls away;
If broadcloth breasts are firmer
Than those of organdy,

Who is to blame? The weaver?
Ah! the bewildering thread!

The tapestries of paradise
So notelessly are made!

LXI

Each life converges to some centre
Expressed or still;
Exists in every human nature
A goal,

Admitted scarcely to itself, it may be,
Too fair
For credibility's temerity
To dare.

Adored with caution, as a brittle heaven,
To reach
Were hopeless as the rainbow's raiment
To touch,

Yet persevered toward, surer for the distance;
How high
Unto the saints' slow diligence
The sky!

Ungained, it may be, by a life's low venture,
But then,
Eternity enables the endeavoring
Again.

LXII

Before I got my eye put out,
I liked as well to see
As other creatures that have eyes,
And know no other way.

But were it told to me, to-day,
That I might have the sky
For mine, I tell you that my heart
Would split, for size of me.

The meadows mine, the mountains mine,—
All forests, stintless stars,
As much of noon as I could take
Between my finite eyes.

The motions of the dipping birds,
The lightning's jointed road,
For mine to look at when I liked,—
The news would strike me dead!

So, safer, guess, with just my soul
Upon the window-pane
Where other creatures put their eyes,
Incautious of the sun.

LXIII

Talk with prudence to a beggar
Of "Potosi" and the mines!
Reverently to the hungry
Of your viands and your wines!

Cautious, hint to any captive
You have passed enfranchised feet!
Anecdotes of air in dungeons
Have sometimes proved deadly sweet!

LXIV

He preached upon "breadth" till it argued him narrow,—
The broad are too broad to define;

And of "truth" until it proclaimed him a liar,—
The truth never flaunted a sign.

Simplicity fled from his counterfeit presence
As gold the pyrites would shun.
What confusion would cover the innocent Jesus
To meet so enabled a man!

LXV

Good night! which put the candle out?
A jealous zephyr, not a doubt.
  Ah! friend, you little knew
How long at that celestial wick
The angels labored diligent;
  Extinguished, now, for you!

It might have been the lighthouse spark
Some sailor, rowing in the dark,
  Had importuned to see!
It might have been the waning lamp
That lit the drummer from the camp
  To purer reveille!

LXVI

When I hoped I feared,
Since I hoped I dared;
Everywhere alone
As a church remain;
Spectre cannot harm,
Serpent cannot charm;
He deposes doom,
Who hath suffered him.

LXVII

A deed knocks first at thought,
And then it knocks at will.
That is the manufacturing spot,
And will at home and well.

It then goes out an act,
Or is entombed so still
That only to the ear of God
Its doom is audible.

LXVIII

Mine enemy is growing old,—
I have at last revenge.
The palate of the hate departs;
If any would avenge,—

Let him be quick, the viand flits,
It is a faded meat.
Anger as soon as fed is dead;
'T is starving makes it fat.

LXIX

Remorse is memory awake,
Her companies astir,—
A presence of departed acts
At window and at door.

Its past set down before the soul,
And lighted with a match,
Perusal to facilitate
Of its condensed despatch.

Remorse is cureless,—the disease
Not even God can heal;
For 't is His institution,—
The complement of hell.

LXX

The body grows outside,—
The more convenient way,—
That if the spirit like to hide,
Its temple stands always

Ajar, secure, inviting;
It never did betray
The soul that asked its shelter
In timid honesty.

LXXI

Undue significance a starving man attaches
To food
Far off; he sighs, and therefore hopeless,
And therefore good.

Partaken, it relieves indeed, but proves us
That spices fly
In the receipt. It was the distance
Was savory.

LXXII

Heart not so heavy as mine,
Wending late home,
As it passed my window
Whistled itself a tune,—

A careless snatch, a ballad,
A ditty of the street;
Yet to my irritated ear
An anodyne so sweet,

It was as if a bobolink,
Sauntering this way,
Carolled and mused and carolled,
Then bubbled slow away.

It was as if a chirping brook
Upon a toilsome way
Set bleeding feet to minuets
Without the knowing why.

To-morrow, night will come again,
Weary, perhaps, and sore.
Ah, bugle, by my window,
I pray you stroll once more!

LXXIII

I many times thought peace had come,
When peace was far away;
As wrecked men deem they sight the land
At centre of the sea,

And struggle slacker, but to prove,
As hopelessly as I,
How many the fictitious shores
Before the harbor lie.

LXXIV

Unto my books so good to turn
Far ends of tired days;

It half endears the abstinence,
And pain is missed in praise.

As flavors cheer retarded guests
With banquetings to be,
So spices stimulate the time
Till my small library.

It may be wilderness without,
Far feet of failing men,
But holiday excludes the night,
And it is bells within.

I thank these kinsmen of the shelf;
Their countenances bland
Enamour in prospective,
And satisfy, obtained.

LXXV

This merit hath the worst,—
It cannot be again.
When Fate hath taunted last
And thrown her furthest stone,

The maimed may pause and breathe,
And glance securely round.
The deer invites no longer
Than it eludes the hound.

LXXVI

I had been hungry all the years;
My noon had come, to dine;
I, trembling, drew the table near,
And touched the curious wine.

'T was this on tables I had seen,
When turning, hungry, lone,
I looked in windows, for the wealth
I could not hope to own.

I did not know the ample bread,
'T was so unlike the crumb
The birds and I had often shared
In Nature's dining-room.

The plenty hurt me, 't was so new,—
Myself felt ill and odd,
As berry of a mountain bush
Transplanted to the road.

Nor was I hungry; so I found
That hunger was a way
Of persons outside windows,
The entering takes away.

LXXVII

I gained it so,
By climbing slow,
By catching at the twigs that grow
Between the bliss and me.
It hung so high,
As well the sky
Attempt by strategy.

I said I gained it,—
This was all.
Look, how I clutch it,
Lest it fall,
And I a pauper go;
Unfitted by an instant's grace

For the contented beggar's face
I wore an hour ago.

LXXVIII

To learn the transport by the pain,
As blind men learn the sun;
To die of thirst, suspecting
That brooks in meadows run;

To stay the homesick, homesick feet
Upon a foreign shore
Haunted by native lands, the while,
And blue, beloved air—

This is the sovereign anguish,
This, the signal woe!
These are the patient laureates
Whose voices, trained below,

Ascend in ceaseless carol,
Inaudible, indeed,
To us, the duller scholars
Of the mysterious bard!

LXXIX

I years had been from home,
And now, before the door,
I dared not open, lest a face
I never saw before

Stare vacant into mine
And ask my business there.
My business,—just a life I left,
Was such still dwelling there?

I fumbled at my nerve,
I scanned the windows near;
The silence like an ocean rolled,
And broke against my ear.

I laughed a wooden laugh
That I could fear a door,
Who danger and the dead had faced,
But never quaked before.

I fitted to the latch
My hand, with trembling care,
Lest back the awful door should spring,
And leave me standing there.

I moved my fingers off
As cautiously as glass,
And held my ears, and like a thief
Fled gasping from the house.

LXXX

Prayer is the little implement
Through which men reach
Where presence is denied them.
They fling their speech

By means of it in God's ear;
If then He hear,
This sums the apparatus
Comprised in prayer.

LXXXI

I know that he exists
Somewhere, in silence.

He has hid his rare life
From our gross eyes.

'T is an instant's play,
'T is a fond ambush,
Just to make bliss
Earn her own surprise!

But should the play
Prove piercing earnest,
Should the glee glaze
In death's stiff stare,

Would not the fun
Look too expensive?
Would not the jest
Have crawled too far?

LXXXII

Musicians wrestle everywhere:
All day, among the crowded air,
  I hear the silver strife;
And—waking long before the dawn—
Such transport breaks upon the town
  I think it that "new life!"

It is not bird, it has no nest;
Nor band, in brass and scarlet dressed,
  Nor tambourine, nor man;
It is not hymn from pulpit read,—
The morning stars the treble led
  On time's first afternoon!

Some say it is the spheres at play!
Some say that bright majority

Of vanished dames and men!
Some think it service in the place
Where we, with late, celestial face,
Please God, shall ascertain!

LXXXIII

Just lost when I was saved!
Just felt the world go by!
Just girt me for the onset with eternity,
When breath blew back,
And on the other side
I heard recede the disappointed tide!

Therefore, as one returned, I feel,
Odd secrets of the line to tell!
Some sailor, skirting foreign shores,
Some pale reporter from the awful doors
Before the seal!

Next time, to stay!
Next time, the things to see
By ear unheard,
Unscrutinized by eye.

Next time, to tarry,
While the ages steal,—
Slow tramp the centuries,
And the cycles wheel.

LXXXIV

'T is little I could care for pearls
Who own the ample sea;
Or brooches, when the Emperor
With rubies pelteth me;

Or gold, who am the Prince of Mines;
  Or diamonds, when I see
A diadem to fit a dome
  Continual crowning me.

LXXXV

Superiority to fate
  Is difficult to learn.
'T is not conferred by any,
  But possible to earn

A pittance at a time,
  Until, to her surprise,
The soul with strict economy
  Subsists till Paradise.

LXXXVI

Hope is a subtle glutton;
  He feeds upon the fair;
And yet, inspected closely,
  What abstinence is there!

His is the halcyon table
  That never seats but one,
And whatsoever is consumed
  The same amounts remain.

LXXXVII

Forbidden fruit a flavor has
  That lawful orchards mocks;
How luscious lies the pea within
  The pod that Duty locks!

LXXXVIII

Heaven is what I cannot reach!
  The apple on the tree,
Provided it do hopeless hang,
  That "heaven" is, to me.

The color on the cruising cloud,
  The interdicted ground
Behind the hill, the house behind,—
  There Paradise is found!

LXXXIX

A word is dead
When it is said,
  Some say.
I say it just
Begins to live
  That day.

XC

To venerate the simple days
  Which lead the seasons by,
Needs but to remember
  That from you or me
They may take the trifle
  Termed mortality!

To invest existence with a stately air,
Needs but to remember
  That the acorn there
Is the egg of forests
  For the upper air!

XCI

It's such a little thing to weep,
 So short a thing to sigh;
And yet by trades the size of these
 We men and women die!

XCII

Drowning is not so pitiful
 As the attempt to rise.
Three times, 't is said, a sinking man
 Comes up to face the skies,
And then declines forever
 To that abhorred abode

Where hope and he part company,—
 For he is grasped of God.
The Maker's cordial visage,
 However good to see,
Is shunned, we must admit it,
 Like an adversity.

XCIII

How still the bells in steeples stand,
 Till, swollen with the sky,
They leap upon their silver feet
 In frantic melody!

XCIV

If the foolish call them "flowers,"
 Need the wiser tell?
If the savants "classify" them,
 It is just as well!

Those who read the *Revelations*
  Must not criticise
Those who read the same edition
  With beclouded eyes!

Could we stand with that old Moses
  Canaan denied,—
Scan, like him, the stately landscape
  On the other side,—

Doubtless we should deem superfluous
  Many sciences
Not pursued by learned angels
  In scholastic skies!

Low amid that glad *Belles lettres*
  Grant that we may stand,
Stars, amid profound Galaxies,
  At that grand "Right hand"!

XCV

Could mortal lip divine
  The undeveloped freight
Of a delivered syllable,
  'T would crumble with the weight.

XCVI

My life closed twice before its close;
  It yet remains to see
If Immortality unveil
  A third event to me,

So huge, so hopeless to conceive,
  As these that twice befell.

Parting is all we know of heaven,
And all we need of hell.

XCVII

We never know how high we are
Till we are called to rise;
And then, if we are true to plan,
Our statures touch the skies.

The heroism we recite
Would be a daily thing,
Did not ourselves the cubits warp
For fear to be a king.

XCVIII

While I was fearing it, it came,
But came with less of fear,
Because that fearing it so long
Had almost made it dear.
There is a fitting—a dismay—
A fitting—a despair.
'T is harder knowing it is due,
Than knowing it is here.
The trying on the utmost,
The morning it is new,
Is terribler than wearing it
A whole existence through.

XCIX

There is no frigate like a book
To take us lands away,
Nor any coursers like a page
Of prancing poetry.

This traverse may the poorest take
  Without oppress of toll;
How frugal is the chariot
  That bears a human soul!

C

Who has not found the heaven below
  Will fail of it above.
God's residence is next to mine,
  His furniture is love.

CI

A face devoid of love or grace,
A hateful, hard, successful face,
  A face with which a stone
Would feel as thoroughly at ease
As were they old acquaintances,—
  First time together thrown.

CII

I had a guinea golden;
  I lost it in the sand,
And though the sum was simple,
  And pounds were in the land,
Still had it such a value
  Unto my frugal eye,
That when I could not find it
  I sat me down to sigh.

I had a crimson robin
  Who sang full many a day,
But when the woods were painted
  He, too, did fly away.

Time brought me other robins,—
  Their ballads were the same,—
Still for my missing troubadour
  I kept the "house at hame."

I had a star in heaven;
  One Pleiad was its name,
And when I was not heeding
  It wandered from the same.
And though the skies are crowded,
  And all the night ashine,
I do not care about it,
  Since none of them are mine.

My story has a moral:
  I have a missing friend,—
Pleiad its name, and robin,
  And guinea in the sand,—
And when this mournful ditty,
  Accompanied with tear,
Shall meet the eye of traitor
  In country far from here,
Grant that repentance solemn
  May seize upon his mind,
And he no consolation
  Beneath the sun may find.

CIII

From all the jails the boys and girls
  Ecstatically leap,—
Beloved, only afternoon
  That prison doesn't keep.

They storm the earth and stun the air,
  A mob of solid bliss.

Alas! that frowns could lie in wait
For such a foe as this!

CIV

Few get enough,—enough is one;
To that ethereal throng
Have not each one of us the right
To stealthily belong?

CV

Upon the gallows hung a wretch,
Too sullied for the hell
To which the law entitled him.
As nature's curtain fell
The one who bore him tottered in,
For this was woman's son.
"'T was all I had," she stricken gasped;
Oh, what a livid boon!

CVI

I felt a cleavage in my mind
As if my brain had split;
I tried to match it, seam by seam,
But could not make them fit.

The thought behind I strove to join
Unto the thought before,
But sequence ravelled out of reach
Like balls upon a floor.

CVII

The reticent volcano keeps
His never slumbering plan;
Confided are his projects pink
To no precarious man.

If nature will not tell the tale
Jehovah told to her,
Can human nature not survive
Without a listener?

Admonished by her buckled lips
Let every babbler be.
The only secret people keep
Is Immortality.

CVIII

If recollecting were forgetting,
Then I remember not;
And if forgetting, recollecting,
How near I had forgot!
And if to miss were merry,
And if to mourn were gay,
How very blithe the fingers
That gathered these to-day!

CIX

The farthest thunder that I heard
Was nearer than the sky,
And rumbles still, though torrid noons
Have lain their missiles by.
The lightning that preceded it
Struck no one but myself,

But I would not exchange the bolt
  For all the rest of life.
Indebtedness to oxygen
  The chemist may repay,
But not the obligation
  To electricity.
It founds the homes and decks the days,
  And every clamor bright
Is but the gleam concomitant
  Of that waylaying light.
The thought is quiet as a flake,—
  A crash without a sound;
How life's reverberation
  Its explanation found!

CX

On the bleakness of my lot
  Bloom I strove to raise.
Late, my acre of a rock
  Yielded grape and maize.

Soil of flint if steadfast tilled
  Will reward the hand;
Seed of palm by Lybian sun
  Fructified in sand.

CXI

A door just opened on a street—
  I, lost, was passing by—
An instant's width of warmth disclosed,
  And wealth, and company.

The door as sudden shut, and I,
  I, lost, was passing by,—

Lost doubly, but by contrast most,
  Enlightening misery.

CXII

Are friends delight or pain?
Could bounty but remain
  Riches were good.

But if they only stay
Bolder to fly away,
  Riches are sad.

CXIII

Ashes denote that fire was;
  Respect the grayest pile
For the departed creature's sake
  That hovered there awhile.

Fire exists the first in light,
  And then consolidates,—
Only the chemist can disclose
  Into what carbonates.

CXIV

Fate slew him, but he did not drop;
  She felled—he did not fall—
Impaled him on her fiercest stakes—
  He neutralized them all.

She stung him, sapped his firm advance,
  But, when her worst was done,
And he, unmoved, regarded her,
  Acknowledged him a man.

CXV

Finite to fail, but infinite to venture.
For the one ship that struts the shore
Many's the gallant, overwhelmed creature
Nodding in navies nevermore.

CXVI

I measure every grief I meet
With analytic eyes;
I wonder if it weighs like mine,
Or has an easier size.

I wonder if they bore it long,
Or did it just begin?
I could not tell the date of mine,
It feels so old a pain.

I wonder if it hurts to live,
And if they have to try,
And whether, could they choose between,
They would not rather die.

I wonder if when years have piled—
Some thousands—on the cause
Of early hurt, if such a lapse
Could give them any pause;

Or would they go on aching still
Through centuries above,
Enlightened to a larger pain
By contrast with the love.

The grieved are many, I am told;
The reason deeper lies,—

Death is but one and comes but once,
   And only nails the eyes.

There's grief of want, and grief of cold,—
   A sort they call "despair";
There's banishment from native eyes,
   In sight of native air.

And though I may not guess the kind
   Correctly, yet to me
A piercing comfort it affords
   In passing Calvary,

To note the fashions of the cross,
   Of those that stand alone,
Still fascinated to presume
   That some are like my own.

CXVII

I have a king who does not speak;
So, wondering, thro' the hours meek
   I trudge the day away,—
Half glad when it is night and sleep,
If, haply, thro' a dream to peep
   In parlors shut by day.

And if I do, when morning comes,
It is as if a hundred drums
   Did round my pillow roll,
And shouts fill all my childish sky,
And bells keep saying "victory"
   From steeples in my soul!

And if I don't, the little Bird
Within the Orchard is not heard,

And I omit to pray,
"Father, thy will be done" to-day,
For my will goes the other way,
And it were perjury!

CXVIII

It dropped so low in my regard
I heard it hit the ground,
And go to pieces on the stones
At bottom of my mind;

Yet blamed the fate that fractured, less
Than I reviled myself
For entertaining plated wares
Upon my silver shelf.

CXIX

To lose one's faith surpasses
The loss of an estate,
Because estates can be
Replenished,—faith cannot.

Inherited with life,
Belief but once can be;
Annihilate a single clause,
And Being's beggary.

CXX

I had a daily bliss
I half indifferent viewed,
Till sudden I perceived it stir,—
It grew as I pursued,

Till when, around a crag,
It wasted from my sight,
Enlarged beyond my utmost scope,
I learned its sweetness right.

CXXI

I worked for chaff, and earning wheat
Was haughty and betrayed.
What right had fields to arbitrate
In matters ratified?

I tasted wheat,—and hated chaff,
And thanked the ample friend;
Wisdom is more becoming viewed
At distance than at hand.

CXXII

Life, and Death, and Giants
Such as these, are still.
Minor apparatus, hopper of the mill,
Beetle at the candle,
Or a fife's small fame,
Maintain by accident
That they proclaim.

CXXIII

Our lives are Swiss,—
So still, so cool,
Till, some odd afternoon,
The Alps neglect their curtains,
And we look farther on.

Italy stands the other side,
While, like a guard between,
The solemn Alps,
The siren Alps,
Forever intervene!

CXXIV

Remembrance has a rear and front,—
'T is something like a house;
It has a garret also
For refuse and the mouse,

Besides, the deepest cellar
That ever mason hewed;
Look to it, by its fathoms
Ourselves be not pursued.

CXXV

To hang our head ostensibly,
And subsequent to find
That such was not the posture
Of our immortal mind,

Affords the sly presumption
That, in so dense a fuzz,
You, too, take cobweb attitudes
Upon a plane of gauze!

CXXVI

The brain is wider than the sky,
For, put them side by side,
The one the other will include
With ease, and you beside.

The brain is deeper than the sea,
For, hold them, blue to blue,
The one the other will absorb,
As sponges, buckets do.

The brain is just the weight of God,
For, lift them, pound for pound,
And they will differ, if they do,
As syllable from sound.

CXXVII

The bone that has no marrow;
What ultimate for that?
It is not fit for table,
For beggar, or for cat.

A bone has obligations,
A being has the same;
A marrowless assembly
Is culpabler than shame.

But how shall finished creatures
A function fresh obtain?—
Old Nicodemus's phantom
Confronting us again!

CXXVIII

The past is such a curious creature,
To look her in the face
A transport may reward us,
Or a disgrace.

Unarmed if any meet her,
I charge him, fly!

Her rusty ammunition
  Might yet reply!

CXXIX

To help our bleaker parts
  Salubrious hours are given,
Which if they do not fit for earth
  Drill silently for heaven.

CXXX

What soft, cherubic creatures
  These gentlewomen are!
One would as soon assault a plush
  Or violate a star.

Such dimity convictions,
  A horror so refined
Of freckled human nature,
  Of Deity ashamed,—

It's such a common glory,
  A fisherman's degree!
Redemption, brittle lady,
  Be so, ashamed of thee.

CXXXI

Who never wanted,—maddest joy
  Remains to him unknown;
The banquet of abstemiousness
  Surpasses that of wine.

Within its hope, though yet ungrasped
  Desire's perfect goal,

No nearer, lest reality
  Should disenthrall thy soul.

CXXXII

It might be easier
  To fail with land in sight,
Than gain my blue peninsula
  To perish of delight.

CXXXIII

You cannot put a fire out;
  A thing that can ignite
Can go, itself, without a fan
  Upon the slowest night.

You cannot fold a flood
  And put it in a drawer,—
Because the winds would find it out,
  And tell your cedar floor.

CXXXIV

A modest lot, a fame *petite*,
A brief campaign of sting and sweet
  Is plenty! Is enough!
A sailor's business is the shore,
  A soldier's—balls. Who asketh more
Must seek the neighboring life!

CXXXV

Is bliss, then, such abyss
I must not put my foot amiss
For fear I spoil my shoe?

I'd rather suit my foot
Than save my boot,
For yet to buy another pair
Is possible
At any fair.

But bliss is sold just once;
The patent lost
None buy it any more.

CXXXVI

I stepped from plank to plank
So slow and cautiously;
The stars about my head I felt,
About my feet the sea.

I knew not but the next
Would be my final inch,—
This gave me that precarious gait
Some call experience.

CXXXVII

One day is there of the series
Termed Thanksgiving day,
Celebrated part at table,
Part in memory.

Neither patriarch nor pussy,
I dissect the play;
Seems it, to my hooded thinking,
Reflex holiday.

Had there been no sharp subtraction
From the early sum,

Not an acre or a caption
  Where was once a room,

Not a mention, whose small pebble
  Wrinkled any bay,—
Unto such, were such assembly,
  'T were Thanksgiving day.

CXXXVIII

Softened by Time's consummate plush,
  How sleek the woe appears
That threatened childhood's citadel
  And undermined the years!

Bisected now by bleaker griefs,
  We envy the despair
That devastated childhood's realm,
  So easy to repair.

PART TWO

Nature

My nosegays are for captives;
Dim, long-expectant eyes,
Fingers denied the plucking,
Patient till paradise.

To such, if they should whisper
Of morning and the moor,
They bear no other errand,
And I, no other prayer.

I

Nature, the gentlest mother,
Impatient of no child,
The feeblest or the waywardest,—
Her admonition mild

In forest and the hill
By traveller is heard,
Restraining rampant squirrel
Or too impetuous bird.

How fair her conversation,
A summer afternoon,—
Her household, her assembly;
And when the sun goes down

Her voice among the aisles
Incites the timid prayer
Of the minutest cricket,
The most unworthy flower.

When all the children sleep
She turns as long away
As will suffice to light her lamps;
Then, bending from the sky,

With infinite affection
And infiniter care,
Her golden finger on her lip,
Wills silence everywhere.

II

Will there really be a morning?
Is there such a thing as day?
Could I see it from the mountains
If I were as tall as they?

Has it feet like water-lilies?
Has it feathers like a bird?
Is it brought from famous countries
Of which I have never heard?

Oh, some scholar! Oh, some sailor!
Oh, some wise man from the skies!
Please to tell a little pilgrim
Where the place called morning lies!

III

At half-past three a single bird
Unto a silent sky
Propounded but a single term
Of cautious melody.

At half-past four, experiment
Had subjugated test,
And lo! her silver principle
Supplanted all the rest.

At half-past seven, element
Nor implement was seen,
And place was where the presence was,
Circumference between.

IV

The day came slow, till five o'clock,
Then sprang before the hills
Like hindered rubies, or the light
A sudden musket spills.

The purple could not keep the east,
The sunrise shook from fold,
Like breadths of topaz, packed a night,
The lady just unrolled.

The happy winds their timbrels took;
The birds, in docile rows,
Arranged themselves around their prince
(The wind is prince of those).

The orchard sparkled like a Jew,—
How mighty 't was, to stay
A guest in this stupendous place,
The parlor of the day!

V

The sun just touched the morning;
The morning, happy thing,
Supposed that he had come to dwell,
And life would be all spring.

She felt herself supremer,—
A raised, ethereal thing;
Henceforth for her what holiday!
Meanwhile, her wheeling king

Trailed slow along the orchards
His haughty, spangled hems,
Leaving a new necessity,—
The want of diadems!

The morning fluttered, staggered,
Felt feebly for her crown,—
Her unanointed forehead
Henceforth her only one.

VI

The robin is the one
That interrupts the morn
With hurried, few, express reports
When March is scarcely on.

The robin is the one
That overflows the noon
With her cherubic quantity,
An April but begun.

The robin is the one
That speechless from her nest
Submits that home and certainty
And sanctity are best.

VII

From cocoon forth a butterfly
As lady from her door
Emerged—a summer afternoon—
Repairing everywhere,

Without design, that I could trace,
Except to stray abroad

On miscellaneous enterprise
The clovers understood.

Her pretty parasol was seen
Contracting in a field
Where men made hay, then struggling hard
With an opposing cloud,

Where parties, phantom as herself,
To Nowhere seemed to go
In purposeless circumference,
As 't were a tropic show.

And notwithstanding bee that worked,
And flower that zealous blew,
This audience of idleness
Disdained them, from the sky,

Till sundown crept, a steady tide,
And men that made the hay,
And afternoon, and butterfly,
Extinguished in its sea.

VIII

Before you thought of spring,
Except as a surmise,
You see, God bless his suddenness,
A fellow in the skies
Of independent hues,
A little weather-worn,
Inspiriting habiliments
Of indigo and brown.

With specimens of song,
As if for you to choose,
Discretion in the interval,
With gay delays he goes
To some superior tree
Without a single leaf,
And shouts for joy to nobody
But his seraphic self!

IX

An altered look about the hills;
A Tyrian light the village fills;
A wider sunrise in the dawn;
A deeper twilight on the lawn;
A print of a vermilion foot;
A purple finger on the slope;
A flippant fly upon the pane;
A spider at his trade again;

An added strut in chanticleer;
A flower expected everywhere;
An axe shrill singing in the woods;
Fern-odors on untravelled roads,—
All this, and more I cannot tell,
A furtive look you know as well,
And Nicodemus's mystery
Receives its annual reply.

X

"Whose are the little beds," I asked,
"Which in the valleys lie?"
Some shook their heads, and others smiled,
And no one made reply.

"Perhaps they did not hear," I said;
"I will inquire again.
Whose are the beds, the tiny beds
So thick upon the plain?"

"'T is daisy in the shortest;
A little farther on,
Nearest the door to wake the first,
Little leontodon.

"'T is iris, sir, and aster,
Anemone and bell,
Batschia in the blanket red,
And chubby daffodil."

Meanwhile at many cradles
Her busy foot she plied,
Humming the quaintest lullaby
That ever rocked a child.

"Hush! Epigea wakens!
The crocus stirs her lids,
Rhodora's cheek is crimson,—
She's dreaming of the woods."

Then, turning from them, reverent,
"Their bed-time 't is," she said;
"The bumble-bees will wake them
When April woods are red."

XI

Pigmy seraphs gone astray,
Velvet people from Vevay,
Belles from some lost summer day,

Bees' exclusive coterie.
Paris could not lay the fold
Belted down with emerald;
Venice could not show a cheek
Of a tint so lustrous meek.
Never such an ambuscade
As of brier and leaf displayed
For my little damask maid.
I had rather wear her grace
Than an earl's distinguished face;
I had rather dwell like her
Than be Duke of Exeter,
Royalty enough for me
To subdue the bumble-bee!

XII

To hear an oriole sing
May be a common thing,
Or only a divine.

It is not of the bird
Who sings the same, unheard,
As unto crowd.

The fashion of the ear
Attireth that it hear
In dun or fair.

So whether it be rune,
Or whether it be none,
Is of within;

The "tune is in the tree,"
The sceptic showeth me;
"No, sir! In thee!"

XIII

One of the ones that Midas touched,
Who failed to touch us all,
Was that confiding prodigal,
The blissful oriole.

So drunk, he disavows it
With badinage divine;
So dazzling, we mistake him
For an alighting mine.

A pleader, a dissembler,
An epicure, a thief,—
Betimes an oratorio,
An ecstasy in chief;

The Jesuit of orchards,
He cheats as he enchants
Of an entire attar
For his decamping wants.

The splendor of a Burmah,
The meteor of birds,
Departing like a pageant
Of ballads and of bards.

I never thought that Jason sought
For any golden fleece;
But then I am a rural man,
With thoughts that make for peace.

But if there were a Jason,
Tradition suffer me
Behold his lost emolument
Upon the apple-tree.

XIV

I dreaded that first robin so,
But he is mastered now,
And I'm accustomed to him grown,—
He hurts a little, though.

I thought if I could only live
Till that first shout got by,
Not all pianos in the woods
Had power to mangle me.

I dared not meet the daffodils,
For fear their yellow gown
Would pierce me with a fashion
So foreign to my own.

I wished the grass would hurry,
So when 't was time to see,
He'd be too tall, the tallest one
Could stretch to look at me.

I could not bear the bees' should come,
I wished they'd stay away
In those dim countries where they go:
What word had they for me?

They're here, though; not a creature failed,
No blossom stayed away
In gentle deference to me,
The Queen of Calvary.

Each one salutes me as he goes,
And I my childish plumes
Lift, in bereaved acknowledgment
Of their unthinking drums.

XV

A route of evanescence
With a revolving wheel;
A resonance of emerald,
A rush of cochineal;
And every blossom on the bush
Adjusts its tumbled head,—
The mail from Tunis, probably,
An easy morning's ride.

XVI

The skies can't keep their secret!
They tell it to the hills—
The hills just tell the orchards—
And they the daffodils!

A bird, by chance, that goes that way
Soft overheard the whole.
If I should bribe the little bird,
Who knows but she would tell?

I think I won't, however,
It's finer not to know;
If summer were an axiom,
What sorcery had snow?

So keep your secret, Father!
I would not, if I could,
Know what the sapphire fellows do,
In your new-fashioned world!

XVII

Who robbed the woods,
The trusting woods?
The unsuspecting trees
Brought out their burrs and mosses
His fantasy to please.
He scanned their trinkets, curious,
He grasped, he bore away.
What will the solemn hemlock,
What will the fir-tree say?

XVIII

Two butterflies went out at noon
And waltzed above a stream,
Then stepped straight through the firmament
And rested on a beam;

And then together bore away
Upon a shining sea,—
Though never yet, in any port,
Their coming mentioned be.

If spoken by the distant bird,
If met in ether sea
By frigate or by merchantman,
Report was not to me.

XIX

I started early, took my dog,
And visited the sea;
The mermaids in the basement
Came out to look at me,

And frigates in the upper floor
Extended hempen hands,
Presuming me to be a mouse
Aground, upon the sands.

But no man moved me till the tide
Went past my simple shoe,
And past my apron and my belt,
And past my bodice too,

And made as he would eat me up
As wholly as a dew
Upon a dandelion's sleeve—
And then I started too.

And he—he followed close behind;
I felt his silver heel
Upon my ankle,—then my shoes
Would overflow with pearl.

Until we met the solid town,
No man he seemed to know;
And bowing with a mighty look
At me, the sea withdrew.

XX

Arcturus is his other name,—
I'd rather call him star!
It's so unkind of science
To go and interfere!

I pull a flower from the woods,—
A monster with a glass
Computes the stamens in a breath,
And has her in a class.

Whereas I took the butterfly
Aforetime in my hat,
He sits erect in cabinets,
The clover-bells forgot.

What once was heaven, is zenith now.
Where I proposed to go
When time's brief masquerade was done,
Is mapped, and charted too!

What if the poles should frisk about
And stand upon their heads!
I hope I'm ready for the worst,
Whatever prank betides!

Perhaps the kingdom of Heaven's changed!
I hope the children there
Won't be new-fashioned when I come,
And laugh at me, and stare!

I hope the father in the skies
Will lift his little girl,—
Old-fashioned, naughty, everything,—
Over the stile of pearl!

XXI

An awful tempest mashed the air,
The clouds were gaunt and few;
A black, as of a spectre's cloak,
Hid heaven and earth from view.

The creatures chuckled on the roofs
And whistled in the air,
And shook their fists and gnashed their teeth,
And swung their frenzied hair.

The morning lit, the birds arose;
The monster's faded eyes
Turned slowly to his native coast,
And peace was Paradise!

XXII

An everywhere of silver,
With ropes of sand
To keep it from effacing
The track called land.

XXIII

A bird came down the walk:
He did not know I saw;
He bit an angle-worm in halves
And ate the fellow, raw.

And then he drank a dew
From a convenient grass,
And then hopped sidewise to the wall
To let a beetle pass.

He glanced with rapid eyes
That hurried all abroad,—
They looked like frightened beads, I thought
He stirred his velvet head

Like one in danger; cautious,
I offered him a crumb,
And he unrolled his feathers
And rowed him softer home

Than oars divide the ocean,
Too silver for a seam,

Or butterflies, off banks of noon,
Leap, plashless, as they swim.

XXIV

A narrow fellow in the grass
Occasionally rides;
You may have met him,—did you not?
His notice sudden is.

The grass divides as with a comb,
A spotted shaft is seen;
And then it closes at your feet
And opens further on.

He likes a boggy acre,
A floor too cool for corn.
Yet when a child, and barefoot,
I more than once, at morn,

Have passed, I thought, a whip-lash
Unbraiding in the sun,—
When, stooping to secure it,
It wrinkled, and was gone.

Several of nature's people
I know, and they know me;
I feel for them a transport
Of cordiality;

But never met this fellow,
Attended or alone,
Without a tighter breathing,
And zero at the bone.

XXV

The mushroom is the elf of plants,
At evening it is not;
At morning in a truffled hut
It stops upon a spot

As if it tarried always;
And yet its whole career
Is shorter than a snake's delay,
And fleeter than a tare.

'T is vegetation's juggler,
The germ of alibi;
Doth like a bubble antedate,
And like a bubble hie.

I feel as if the grass were pleased
To have it intermit;
The surreptitious scion
Of summer's circumspect.

Had nature any outcast face,
Could she a son contemn,
Had nature an Iscariot,
That mushroom,—it is him.

XXVI

There came a wind like a bugle;
It quivered through the grass,
And a green chill upon the heat
So ominous did pass
We barred the windows and the doors
As from an emerald ghost;
The doom's electric moccason

That very instant passed.
On a strange mob of panting trees,
And fences fled away,
And rivers where the houses ran
The living looked that day.
The bell within the steeple wild
The flying tidings whirled.
How much can come
And much can go,
And yet abide the world!

XXVII

A spider sewed at night
Without a light
Upon an arc of white.
If ruff it was of dame
Or shroud of gnome,
Himself, himself inform.
Of immortality
His strategy
Was physiognomy.

XXVIII

I know a place where summer strives
With such a practised frost,
She each year leads her daisies back,
Recording briefly, "Lost."

But when the south wind stirs the pools
And struggles in the lanes,
Her heart misgives her for her vow,
And she pours soft refrains

Into the lap of adamant,
And spices, and the dew,
That stiffens quietly to quartz,
Upon her amber shoe.

XXIX

The one that could repeat the summer day
Were greater than itself, though he
Minutest of mankind might be.
And who could reproduce the sun,
At period of going down—
The lingering and the stain, I mean—
When Orient has been outgrown,
And Occident becomes unknown,
His name remain.

XXX

The wind tapped like a tired man,
And like a host, "Come in,"
I boldly answered; entered then
My residence within

A rapid, footless guest,
To offer whom a chair
Were as impossible as hand
A sofa to the air.

No bone had he to bind him,
His speech was like the push
Of numerous humming-birds at once
From a superior bush.

His countenance a billow,
His fingers, if he pass,

Let go a music, as of tunes
Blown tremulous in glass.

He visited, still flitting;
Then, like a timid man,
Again he tapped—'t was flurriedly—
And I became alone.

XXXI

Nature rarer uses yellow
  Than another hue;
Saves she all of that for sunsets,—
  Prodigal of blue,

Spending scarlet like a woman,
  Yellow she affords
Only scantly and selectly,
  Like a lover's words.

XXXII

The leaves, like women, interchange
  Sagacious confidence;
Somewhat of nods, and somewhat of
  Portentous inference,

The parties in both cases
  Enjoining secrecy,—
Inviolable compact
  To notoriety.

XXXIII

How happy is the little stone
That rambles in the road alone,

And does n't care about careers,
And exigencies never fears;
Whose coat of elemental brown
A passing universe put on;
And independent as the sun,
Associates or glows alone,
Fulfilling absolute decree
In casual simplicity.

XXXIV

It sounded as if the streets were running,
And then the streets stood still.
Eclipse was all we could see at the window,
And awe was all we could feel.

By and by the boldest stole out of his covert,
To see if time was there.
Nature was in her beryl apron,
Mixing fresher air.

XXXV

The rat is the concisest tenant.
He pays no rent,—
Repudiates the obligation,
On schemes intent.

Balking our wit
To sound or circumvent,
Hate cannot harm
A foe so reticent.

Neither decree
Prohibits him,

Lawful as
Equilibrium.

XXXVI

Frequently the woods are pink,
Frequently are brown;
Frequently the hills undress
Behind my native town.

Oft a head is crested
I was wont to see,
And as oft a cranny
Where it used to be.

And the earth, they tell me,
On its axis turned,—
Wonderful rotation
By but twelve performed!

XXXVII

The wind began to rock the grass
With threatening tunes and low,—
He flung a menace at the earth,
A menace at the sky.

The leaves unhooked themselves from trees
And started all abroad;
The dust did scoop itself like hands
And throw away the road.

The wagons quickened on the streets,
The thunder hurried slow;
The lightning showed a yellow beak,
And then a livid claw.

The birds put up the bars to nests,
The cattle fled to barns;
There came one drop of giant rain,
And then, as if the hands

That held the dams had parted hold,
The waters wrecked the sky,
But overlooked my father's house,
Just quartering a tree.

XXXVIII

South winds jostle them,
Bumblebees come,
Hover, hesitate,
Drink, and are gone.

Butterflies pause
On their passage Cashmere;
I, softly plucking,
Present them here!

XXXIX

Bring me the sunset in a cup,
Reckon the morning's flagons up,
  And say how many dew;
Tell me how far the morning leaps,
Tell me what time the weaver sleeps
  Who spun the breadths of blue!

Write me how many notes there be
In the new robin's ecstasy
  Among astonished boughs;
How many trips the tortoise makes,

How many cups the bee partakes,—
 The debauchee of dews!

Also, who laid the rainbow's piers,
Also, who leads the docile spheres
 By withes of supple blue?
Whose fingers string the stalactite,
Who counts the wampum of the night,
 To see that none is due?

Who built this little Alban house
And shut the windows down so close
 My spirit cannot see?
Who'll let me out some gala day,
With implements to fly away,
 Passing pomposity?

XL

She sweeps with many-colored brooms,
And leaves the shreds behind;
Oh, housewife in the evening west,
Come back, and dust the pond!

You dropped a purple ravelling in,
You dropped an amber thread;
And now you've littered all the East
With duds of emerald!

And still she plies her spotted brooms,
And still the aprons fly,
Till brooms fade softly into stars—
And then I come away.

XLI

Like mighty footlights burned the red
At bases of the trees,—
The far theatricals of day
Exhibiting to these.

'T was universe that did applaud
While, chiefest of the crowd,
Enabled by his royal dress,
Myself distinguished God.

XLII

Where ships of purple gently toss
On seas of daffodil,
Fantastic sailors mingle,
And then—the wharf is still.

XLIII

Blazing in gold and quenching in purple,
Leaping like leopards to the sky,
Then at the feet of the old horizon
Laying her spotted face, to die;

Stooping as low as the kitchen window,
Touching the roof and tinting the barn,
Kissing her bonnet to the meadow,—
And the juggler of day is gone!

XLIV

Farther in summer than the birds,
Pathetic from the grass,

A minor nation celebrates
Its unobtrusive mass.

No ordinance is seen,
So gradual the grace,
A pensive custom it becomes,
Enlarging loneliness.

Antiquest felt at noon
When August, burning low,
Calls forth this spectral canticle,
Repose to typify.

Remit as yet no grace,
No furrow on the glow,
Yet a druidic difference
Enhances nature now.

XLV

As imperceptibly as grief
The summer lapsed away,—
Too imperceptible, at last,
To seem like perfidy.

A quietness distilled,
As twilight long begun,
Or Nature, spending with herself
Sequestered afternoon.

The dusk drew earlier in,
The morning foreign shone,—
A courteous, yet harrowing grace,
As guest who would be gone.

And thus, without a wing,
Or service of a keel,
Our summer made her light escape
Into the beautiful.

XLVI

It can't be summer,—that got through;
It's early yet for spring;
There's that long town of white to cross
Before the blackbirds sing.

It can't be dying,—it's too rouge,—
The dead shall go in white.
So sunset shuts my question down
With clasps of chrysolite.

XLVII

The gentian weaves her fringes,
The maple's loom is red.
My departing blossoms
Obviate parade.

A brief, but patient illness,
An hour to prepare;
And one, below this morning,
Is where the angels are.

It was a short procession,—
The bobolink was there,
An aged bee addressed us,
And then we knelt in prayer.

We trust that she was willing,—
We ask that we may be.

Summer, sister, seraph,
Let us go with thee!

In the name of the bee
And of the butterfly
And of the breeze, amen!

XLVIII

God made a little gentian;
It tried to be a rose
And failed, and all the summer laughed.
But just before the snows
There came a purple creature
That ravished all the hill;
And summer hid her forehead,
And mockery was still.
The frosts were her condition;
The Tyrian would not come
Until the North evoked it.
"Creator! shall I bloom?"

XLIX

Besides the autumn poets sing,
A few prosaic days
A little this side of the snow
And that side of the haze.

A few incisive mornings,
A few ascetic eves,—
Gone Mr. Bryant's golden-rod,
And Mr. Thomson's sheaves.

Still is the bustle in the brook,
Sealed are the spicy valves;

Mesmeric fingers softly touch
The eyes of many elves.

Perhaps a squirrel may remain,
My sentiments to share.
Grant me, O Lord, a sunny mind,
Thy windy will to bear!

L

It sifts from leaden sieves,
It powders all the wood,
It fills with alabaster wool
The wrinkles of the road.

It makes an even face
Of mountain and of plain,—
Unbroken forehead from the east
Unto the east again.

It reaches to the fence,
It wraps it, rail by rail,
Till it is lost in fleeces;
It flings a crystal veil

On stump and stack and stem,—
The summer's empty room,
Acres of seams where harvests were,
Recordless, but for them.

It ruffles wrists of posts,
As ankles of a queen,—
Then stills its artisans like ghosts,
Denying they have been.

LI

No brigadier throughout the year
So civic as the Jay.
A neighbor and a warrior too,
With shrill felicity

Pursuing winds that censure us
A February day,
The brother of the universe
Was never blown away.

The snow and he are intimate;
I've often seen them play
When heaven looked upon us all
With such severity,

I felt apology were due
To an insulted sky,
Whose pompous frown was nutriment
To their temerity.

The pillow of this daring head
Is pungent evergreens;
His larder—terse and militant—
Unknown, refreshing things;

His character a tonic,
His future a dispute;
Unfair an immortality
That leaves this neighbor out.

LII

New feet within my garden go,
New fingers stir the sod;

A troubadour upon the elm
Betrays the solitude.

New children play upon the green,
New weary sleep below;
And still the pensive spring returns,
And still the punctual snow!

LIII

Pink, small, and punctual.
Aromatic, low,
Covert in April,
Candid in May,

Dear to the moss,
Known by the knoll,
Next to the robin
In every human soul.

Bold little beauty.
Bedecked with thee,
Nature forswears
Antiquity.
(With the first Arbutus.)

LIV

The murmur of a bee
A witchcraft yieldeth me.
If any ask me why.
'T were easier to die
Than tell.

The red upon the hill
Taketh away my will:

If anybody sneer,
Take care, for God is here,
That's all.

The breaking of the day
Addeth to my degree;
If any ask me how,
Artist, who drew me so,
Must tell!

LV

Perhaps you'd like to buy a flower?
But I could never sell.
If you would like to borrow
Until the daffodil

Unties her yellow bonnet
Beneath the village door,
Until the bees, from clover rows
Their hock and sherry draw,

Why, I will lend until just then,
But not an hour more!

LVI

The pedigree of honey
Does not concern the bee;
A clover, any time, to him
Is aristocracy.

LVII

Some keep the Sabbath going to church;
I keep it staying at home,

With a bobolink for a chorister,
And an orchard for a dome.

Some keep the Sabbath in surplice;
I just wear my wings,
And instead of tolling the bell for church,
Our little sexton sings.

God preaches,—a noted clergyman,—
And the sermon is never long;
So instead of getting to heaven at last,
I'm going all along!

LVIII

The bee is not afraid of me,
I know the butterfly;
The pretty people in the woods
Receive me cordially.

The brooks laugh louder when I come,
The breezes madder play.
Wherefore, mine eyes, thy silver mists?
Wherefore, O summer's day?

LIX

Some rainbow coming from the fair!
Some vision of the World Cashmere
I confidently see!
Or else a peacock's purple train,
Feather by feather, on the plain
Fritters itself away!

The dreamy butterflies bestir,
Lethargic pools resume the whir

Of last year's sundered tune.
From some old fortress on the sun
Baronial bees march, one by one,
In murmuring platoon!

The robins stand as thick to-day
As flakes of snow stood yesterday,
On fence and roof and twig.
The orchis binds her feather on
For her old lover, Don the Sun,
Revisiting the bog!

Without commander, countless, still,
The regiment of wood and hill
In bright detachment stand.
Behold! Whose multitudes are these?
The children of whose turbaned seas,
Or what Circassian land?

LX

The grass so little has to do,—
A sphere of simple green,
With only butterflies to brood,
And bees to entertain,

And stir all day to pretty tunes
The breezes fetch along,
And hold the sunshine in its lap
And bow to everything;

And thread the dews all night, like pearls,
And make itself so fine,—
A duchess were too common
For such a noticing.

And even when it dies, to pass
In odors so divine,
As lowly spices gone to sleep,
Or amulets of pine.

And then to dwell in sovereign barns,
And dream the days away,—
The grass so little has to do,
I wish I were a hay!

LXI

A little road not made of man,
Enabled of the eye,
Accessible to thill of bee,
Or cart of butterfly.

If town it have, beyond itself,
'T is that I cannot say;
I only sigh,—no vehicle
Bears me along that way.

LXII

A drop fell on the apple tree.
Another on the roof;
A half a dozen kissed the eaves,
And made the gables laugh.

A few went out to help the brook,
That went to help the sea.
Myself conjectured, Were they pearls,
What necklaces could be!

The dust replaced in hoisted roads,
The birds jocoser sung;

The sunshine threw his hat away,
The orchards spangles hung.

The breezes brought dejected lutes,
And bathed them in the glee;
The East put out a single flag,
And signed the fête away.

LXIII

A something in a summer's day,
As slow her flambeaux burn away,
Which solemnizes me.

A something in a summer's noon,—
An azure depth, a wordless tune,
Transcending ecstasy.

And still within a summer's night
A something so transporting bright,
I clap my hands to see;

Then veil my too inspecting face,
Lest such a subtle, shimmering grace
Flutter too far for me.

The wizard-fingers never rest,
The purple brook within the breast
Still chafes its narrow bed;

Still rears the East her amber flag,
Guides still the sun along the crag
His caravan of red,

Like flowers that heard the tale of dews,
But never deemed the dripping prize
Awaited their low brows;

Or bees, that thought the summer's name
Some rumor of delirium
No summer could for them;

Or Arctic creature, dimly stirred
By tropic hint,—some travelled bird
Imported to the wood;

Or wind's bright signal to the ear,
Making that homely and severe,
Contented, known, before

The heaven unexpected came,
To lives that thought their worshipping
A too presumptuous psalm.

LXIV

This is the land the sunset washes,
These are the banks of the Yellow Sea;
Where it rose, or whither it rushes,
These are the western mystery!

Night after night her purple traffic
Strews the landing with opal bales;
Merchantmen poise upon horizons,
Dip, and vanish with fairy sails.

LXV

Like trains of cars on tracks of plush
I hear the level bee:

A jar across the flowers goes,
Their velvet masonry

Withstands until the sweet assault
Their chivalry consumes,
While he, victorious, tilts away
To vanquish other blooms.

His feet are shod with gauze,
His helmet is of gold;
His breast, a single onyx
With chrysoprase, inlaid.

His labor is a chant,
His idleness a tune;
Oh, for a bee's experience
Of clovers and of noon!

LXVI

There is a flower that bees prefer,
And butterflies desire;
To gain the purple democrat
The humming-birds aspire.

And whatsoever insect pass,
A honey bears away
Proportioned to his several dearth
And her capacity.

Her face is rounder than the moon,
And ruddier than the gown
Of orchis in the pasture,
Or rhododendron worn.

She doth not wait for June;
Before the world is green
Her sturdy little countenance
Against the wind is seen,

Contending with the grass,
Near kinsman to herself,
For privilege of sod and sun,
Sweet litigants for life.

And when the hills are full,
And newer fashions blow,
Doth not retract a single spice
For pang of jealousy.

Her public is the noon,
Her providence the sun,
Her progress by the bee proclaimed
In sovereign, swerveless tune.

The bravest of the host,
Surrendering the last,
Nor even of defeat aware
When cancelled by the frost.

LXVII

Presentiment is that long shadow on the lawn
Indicative that suns go down;
The notice to the startled grass
That darkness is about to pass.

LXVIII

As children bid the guest good-night,
And then reluctant turn,
My flowers raise their pretty lips,
Then put their nightgowns on.

As children caper when they wake,
Merry that it is morn,
My flowers from a hundred cribs
Will peep, and prance again.

LXIX

Angels in the early morning
May be seen the dews among,
Stooping, plucking, smiling, flying:
Do the buds to them belong?

Angels when the sun is hottest
May be seen the sands among,
Stooping, plucking, sighing, flying;
Parched the flowers they bear along.

LXX

So bashful when I spied her,
So pretty, so ashamed!
So hidden in her leaflets,
Lest anybody find;

So breathless till I passed her,
So helpless when I turned
And bore her, struggling, blushing,
Her simple haunts beyond!

For whom I robbed the dingle,
For whom betrayed the dell,
Many will doubtless ask me,
But I shall never tell!

LXXI

It makes no difference abroad,
The seasons fit the same,
The mornings blossom into noons,
And split their pods of flame.

Wild-flowers kindle in the woods,
The brooks brag all the day;
No blackbird bates his jargoning
For passing Calvary.

Auto-da-fé and judgment
Are nothing to the bee;
His separation from his rose
To him seems misery.

LXXII

The mountain sat upon the plain
In his eternal chair,
His observation omnifold,
His inquest everywhere.

The seasons prayed around his knees,
Like children round a sire:
Grandfather of the days is he,
Of dawn the ancestor.

LXXIII

I'll tell you how the sun rose,—
A ribbon at a time.
The steeples swam in amethyst,
The news like squirrels ran.

The hills untied their bonnets,
The bobolinks begun.
Then I said softly to myself,
"That must have been the sun!"

* * * * * *

But how he set, I know not.
There seemed a purple stile
Which little yellow boys and girls
Were climbing all the while

Till when they reached the other side,
A dominie in gray
Put gently up the evening bars,
And led the flock away.

LXXIV

The butterfly's assumption-gown,
In chrysoprase apartments hung,
  This afternoon put on.

How condescending to descend,
And be of buttercups the friend
  In a New England town!

LXXV

Of all the sounds despatched abroad,
There's not a charge to me
Like that old measure in the boughs,
That phraseless melody

The wind does, working like a hand
Whose fingers comb the sky,
Then quiver down, with tufts of tune
Permitted gods and me.

When winds go round and round in bands,
And thrum upon the door,
And birds take places overhead,
To bear them orchestra,

I crave him grace, of summer boughs,
If such an outcast be,
He never heard that fleshless chant
Rise solemn in the tree,

As if some caravan of sound
On deserts, in the sky,
Had broken rank,
Then knit, and passed
In seamless company.

LXXVI

Apparently with no surprise
To any happy flower,
The frost beheads it at its play
In accidental power.

The blond assassin passes on,
The sun proceeds unmoved
To measure off another day
For an approving God.

LXXVII

'T was later when the summer went
Than when the cricket came,
And yet we knew that gentle clock
Meant nought but going home.

'T was sooner when the cricket went
Than when the winter came,
Yet that pathetic pendulum
Keeps esoteric time.

LXXVIII

These are the days when birds come back,
A very few, a bird or two,
To take a backward look.

These are the days when skies put on
The old, old sophistries of June,—
A blue and gold mistake.

Oh, fraud that cannot cheat the bee,
Almost thy plausibility
Induces my belief,

Till ranks of seeds their witness bear,
And softly through the altered air
Hurries a timid leaf!

Oh, sacrament of summer days,
Oh, last communion in the haze,
Permit a child to join,

Thy sacred emblems to partake,
Thy consecrated bread to break,
Taste thine immortal wine!

LXXIX

The morns are meeker than they were,
The nuts are getting brown;
The berry's cheek is plumper,
The rose is out of town.

The maple wears a gayer scarf,
The field a scarlet gown.
Lest I should be old-fashioned,
I'll put a trinket on.

LXXX

The sky is low, the clouds are mean,
A travelling flake of snow
Across a barn or through a rut
Debates if it will go.

A narrow wind complains all day
How some one treated him;
Nature, like us, is sometimes caught
Without her diadem.

LXXXI

I think the hemlock likes to stand
Upon a marge of snow;

It suits his own austerity,
And satisfies an awe

That men must slake in wilderness,
Or in the desert cloy,—
An instinct for the hoar, the bald,
Lapland's necessity.

The hemlock's nature thrives on cold;
The gnash of northern winds
Is sweetest nutriment to him,
His best Norwegian wines.

To satin races he is nought;
But children on the Don
Beneath his tabernacles play,
And Dnieper wrestlers run.

LXXXII

There's a certain slant of light,
On winter afternoons,
That oppresses, like the weight
Of cathedral tunes.

Heavenly hurt it gives us;
We can find no scar,
But internal difference
Where the meanings are.

None may teach it anything,
'T is the seal, despair,—
An imperial affliction
Sent us of the air.

When it comes, the landscape listens,
Shadows hold their breath;
When it goes, 't is like the distance
On the look of death.

LXXXIII

The springtime's pallid landscape
  Will glow like bright bouquet,
Though drifted deep in parian
  The village lies to-day.

The lilacs, bending many a year,
  With purple load will hang;
The bees will not forget the tune
  Their old forefathers sang.

The rose will redden in the bog,
  The aster on the hill
Her everlasting fashion set,
  And covenant gentians frill,

Till summer folds her miracle
  As women do their gown,
Or priests adjust the symbols
  When sacrament is done.

LXXXIV

She slept beneath a tree
Remembered but by me.
I touched her cradle mute;
She recognized the foot,
Put on her carmine suit,—
  And see!

(With a Tulip.)

LXXXV

A light exists in spring
  Not present on the year
At any other period.
  When March is scarcely here

A color stands abroad
  On solitary hills
That science cannot overtake,
  But human nature *feels*.

It waits upon the lawn;
  It shows the furthest tree
Upon the furthest slope we know;
  It almost speaks to me.

Then, as horizons step,
  Or noons report away,
Without the formula of sound,
  It passes, and we stay:

A quality of loss
  Affecting our content,
As trade had suddenly encroached
  Upon a sacrament.

LXXXVI

A lady red upon the hill
  Her annual secret keeps;
A lady white within the field
  In placid lily sleeps!

The tidy breezes with their brooms
  Sweep vale, and hill, and tree!

Prithee, my pretty housewives!
  Who may expected be?

The neighbors do not yet suspect!
  The woods exchange a smile—
Orchard, and buttercup, and bird—
  In such a little while!

And yet how still the landscape stands,
  How nonchalant the wood,
As if the resurrection
  Were nothing very odd!

LXXXVII

Dear March, come in!
How glad I am!
I looked for you before.
Put down your hat—
You must have walked—
How out of breath you are!
Dear March, how are you?
And the rest?
Did you leave Nature well?
Oh, March, come right upstairs with me,
I have so much to tell!

I got your letter, and the bird's;
The maples never knew
That you were coming,—I declare,
How red their faces grew!
But, March, forgive me—
And all those hills
You left for me to hue;
There was no purple suitable,
You took it all with you.

Who knocks? That April!
Lock the door!
I will not be pursued!
He stayed away a year, to call
When I am occupied.
But trifles look so trivial
As soon as you have come,
That blame is just as dear as praise
And praise as mere as blame.

LXXXVIII

We like March, his shoes are purple,
  He is new and high;
Makes he mud for dog and peddler,
  Makes he forest dry;
Knows the adder's tongue his coming,
  And begets her spot.
Stands the sun so close and mighty
  That our minds are hot.
News is he of all the others;
  Bold it were to die
With the blue-birds buccaneering
  On his British sky.

LXXXIX

Not knowing when the dawn will come
  I open every door;
Or has it feathers like a bird,
  Or billows like a shore?

XC

A murmur in the trees to note,
  Not loud enough for wind;

A star not far enough to seek,
   Nor near enough to find;

A long, long yellow on the lawn,
   A hubbub as of feet;
Not audible, as ours to us,
   But dapperer, more sweet;

A hurrying home of little men
   To houses unperceived,—
All this, and more, if I should tell,
   Would never be believed.

Of robins in the trundle bed
   How many I espy
Whose nightgowns could not hide the wings,
   Although I heard them try!

But then I promised ne'er to tell;
   How could I break my word?
So go your way and I'll go mine,—
   No fear you'll miss the road.

XCI

Morning is the place for dew,
   Corn is made at noon,
After dinner light for flowers,
   Dukes for setting sun!

XCII

To my quick ear the leaves conferred;
   The bushes they were bells;
I could not find a privacy
   From Nature's sentinels.

In cave if I presumed to hide,
  The walls began to tell;
Creation seemed a mighty crack
  To make me visible.

XCIII

A sepal, petal, and a thorn
Upon a common summer's morn,
A flash of dew, a bee or two,
A breeze
A caper in the trees,—
  And I'm a rose!

XCIV

High from the earth I heard a bird;
  He trod upon the trees
As he esteemed them trifles,
  And then he spied a breeze,
And situated softly
  Upon a pile of wind
Which in a perturbation
  Nature had left behind.
A joyous-going fellow
  I gathered from his talk,
Which both of benediction
  And badinage partook,
Without apparent burden,
  I learned, in leafy wood
He was the faithful father
  Of a dependent brood;
And this untoward transport
  His remedy for care,—
A contrast to our respites.
  How different we are!

XCV

The spider as an artist
  Has never been employed
Though his surpassing merit
  Is freely certified

By every broom and Bridget
  Throughout a Christian land.
Neglected son of genius,
  I take thee by the hand.

XCVI

What mystery pervades a well!
  The water lives so far,
Like neighbor from another world
  Residing in a jar.

The grass does not appear afraid;
  I often wonder he
Can stand so close and look so bold
  At what is dread to me.

Related somehow they may be,—
  The sedge stands next the sea,
Where he is floorless, yet of fear
  No evidence gives he.

But nature is a stranger yet;
  The ones that cite her most
Have never passed her haunted house,
  Nor simplified her ghost.

To pity those that know her not
  Is helped by the regret

That those who know her, know her less
The nearer her they get.

XCVII

To make a prairie it takes a clover
and one bee,—
One clover, and a bee,
And revery.
The revery alone will do
If bees are few.

XCVIII

It's like the light,—
A fashionless delight,
It's like the bee,—
A dateless melody.

It's like the woods,
Private like breeze,
Phraseless, yet it stirs
The proudest trees.

It's like the morning,—
Best when it's done,—
The everlasting clocks
Chime noon.

XCIX

A dew sufficed itself
And satisfied a leaf,
And felt, "how vast a destiny!
How trivial is life!"

The sun went out to work,
  The day went out to play,
But not again that dew was seen
  By physiognomy.

Whether by day abducted,
  Or emptied by the sun
Into the sea, in passing,
  Eternally unknown.

C

His bill an auger is,
  His head, a cap and frill.
He laboreth at every tree,—
  A worm his utmost goal.

CI

Sweet is the swamp with its secrets,
  Until we meet a snake;
'T is then we sigh for houses,
  And our departure take

At that enthralling gallop
  That only childhood knows.
A snake is summer's treason,
  And guile is where it goes.

CII

Could I but ride indefinite,
  As doth the meadow-bee,
And visit only where I liked,
  And no man visit me,

And flirt all day with buttercups,
And marry whom I may,
And dwell a little everywhere,
Or better, run away

With no police to follow,
Or chase me if I do,
Till I should jump peninsulas
To get away from you,—

I said, but just to be a bee
Upon a raft of air,
And row in nowhere all day long,
And anchor off the bar,—
What liberty! So captives deem
Who tight in dungeons are.

CIII

The moon was but a chin of gold
A night or two ago,
And now she turns her perfect face
Upon the world below.

Her forehead is of amplest blond;
Her cheek like beryl stone;
Her eye unto the summer dew
The likest I have known.

Her lips of amber never part;
But what must be the smile
Upon her friend she could bestow
Were such her silver will!

And what a privilege to be
But the remotest star!

For certainly her way might pass
Beside your twinkling door.

Her bonnet is the firmament,
The universe her shoe,
The stars the trinkets at her belt,
Her dimities of blue.

CIV

The bat is dun with wrinkled wings
Like fallow article,
And not a song pervades his lips,
Or none perceptible.

His small umbrella, quaintly halved,
Describing in the air
An arc alike inscrutable,—
Elate philosopher!

Deputed from what firmament
Of what astute abode,
Empowered with what malevolence
Auspiciously withheld.

To his adroit Creator
Ascribe no less the praise;
Beneficent, believe me,
His eccentricities.

CV

You've seen balloons set, haven't you?
So stately they ascend
It is as swans discarded you
For duties diamond.

Their liquid feet go softly out
  Upon a sea of blond;
They spurn the air as 't were to mean
  For creatures so renowned.

Their ribbons just beyond the eye,
  They struggle some for breath,
And yet the crowd applauds below;
  They would not encore death.

The gilded creature strains and spins,
  Trips frantic in a tree,
Tears open her imperial veins
  And tumbles in the sea.

The crowd retire with an oath
  The dust in streets goes down,
And clerks in counting-rooms observe,
  "'T was only a balloon."

CVI

The cricket sang,
  And set the sun,
And workmen finished, one by one,
  Their seam the day upon.

The low grass loaded with the dew,
The twilight stood as strangers do
With hat in hand, polite and new,
  To stay as if, or go.

A vastness, as a neighbor, came,—
A wisdom without face or name,
A peace, as hemispheres at home,—
  And so the night became.

CVII

Drab habitation of whom?
Tabernacle or tomb,
Or dome of worm,
Or porch of gnome,
Or some elf's catacomb?
(Sent with a cocoon to her little nephew.)

CVIII

A sloop of amber slips away
 Upon an ether sea,
And wrecks in peace a purple tar,
 The son of ecstasy.

CIX

Of bronze and blaze
The north, to-night!
 So adequate its forms,
So preconcerted with itself,
 So distant to alarms,—
An unconcern so sovereign
 To universe, or me,
It paints my simple spirit
 With tints of majesty,
Till I take vaster attitudes,
 And strut upon my stem,
Disdaining men and oxygen,
 For arrogance of them.

My splendors are menagerie;
 But their competeless show
Will entertain the centuries
 When I am, long ago,

An island in dishonored grass,
  Whom none but daisies know.

CX

How the old mountains drip with sunset,
  And the brake of dun!
How the hemlocks are tipped in tinsel
  By the wizard sun!

How the old steeples hand the scarlet,
  Till the ball is full,—
Have I the lip of the flamingo
  That I dare to tell?

Then, how the fire ebbs like billows,
  Touching all the grass
With a departing, sapphire feature,
  As if a duchess pass!

How a small dusk crawls on the village
  Till the houses blot;
And the odd flambeaux no men carry
  Glimmer on the spot!

Now it is night in nest and kennel,
  And where was the wood,
Just a dome of abyss is nodding
  Into solitude!—

These are the visions baffled Guido;
  Titian never told;
Domenichino dropped the pencil,
  Powerless to unfold.

CXI

The murmuring of bees has ceased;
  But murmuring of some
Posterior, prophetic,
  Has simultaneous come,—

The lower metres of the year,
  When nature's laugh is done,—
The Revelations of the book
  Whose Genesis is June.

PART THREE

Love

It's all I have to bring to-day,
This, and my heart beside,
This, and my heart, and all the fields,
And all the meadows wide.
Be sure you count, should I forget,—
Some one the sun could tell,—
This, and my heart, and all the bees
Which in the clover dwell.

I

Mine by the right of the white election!
Mine by the royal seal!
Mine by the sign in the scarlet prison
Bars cannot conceal!

Mine, here in vision and in veto!
Mine, by the grave's repeal
Titled, confirmed,—delirious charter!
Mine, while the ages steal!

II

You left me, sweet, two legacies,—
A legacy of love
A Heavenly Father would content,
Had He the offer of;

You left me boundaries of pain
Capacious as the sea,
Between eternity and time,
Your consciousness and me.

III

Alter? When the hills do.
Falter? When the sun
Question if his glory
Be the perfect one.

Surfeit? When the daffodil
Doth of the dew:
Even as herself, O friend!
I will of you!

IV

Elysium is as far as to
The very nearest room,
If in that room a friend await
Felicity or doom.

What fortitude the soul contains,
That it can so endure
The accent of a coming foot,
The opening of a door!

V

Doubt me, my dim companion!
Why, God would be content
With but a fraction of the love
Poured thee without a stint.
The whole of me, forever,
What more the woman can,—
Say quick, that I may dower thee
With last delight I own!

It cannot be my spirit,
For that was thine before;
I ceded all of dust I knew,—
What opulence the more
Had I, a humble maiden,
Whose farthest of degree
Was that she might

Some distant heaven,
Dwell timidly with thee!

VI

If you were coming in the fall,
I'd brush the summer by
With half a smile and half a spurn,
As housewives do a fly.

If I could see you in a year,
I'd wind the months in balls,
And put them each in separate drawers,
Until their time befalls.

If only centuries delayed,
I'd count them on my hand,
Subtracting till my fingers dropped
Into Van Diemen's land.

If certain, when this life was out,
That yours and mine should be,
I'd toss it yonder like a rind,
And taste eternity.

But now, all ignorant of the length
Of time's uncertain wing,
It goads me, like the goblin bee,
That will not state its sting.

VII

I hide myself within my flower,
That wearing on your breast,
You, unsuspecting, wear me too—
And angels know the rest.

I hide myself within my flower,
That, fading from your vase,
You, unsuspecting, feel for me
Almost a loneliness.

VIII

That I did always love,
I bring thee proof:
That till I loved
I did not love enough.

That I shall love always,
I offer thee
That love is life,
And life hath immortality.

This, dost thou doubt, sweet?
Then have I
Nothing to show
But Calvary.

IX

Have you got a brook in your little heart,
Where bashful flowers blow,
And blushing birds go down to drink,
And shadows tremble so?

And nobody knows, so still it flows,
That any brook is there;
And yet your little draught of life
Is daily drunken there.

Then look out for the little brook in March,
When the rivers overflow,

And the snows come hurrying from the hills,
And the bridges often go.

And later, in August it may be,
When the meadows parching lie,
Beware, lest this little brook of life
Some burning noon go dry!

X

As if some little Arctic flower,
Upon the polar hem,
Went wandering down the latitudes,
Until it puzzled came
To continents of summer,
To firmaments of sun,
To strange, bright crowds of flowers,
And birds of foreign tongue!
I say, as if this little flower
To Eden wandered in—
What then? Why, nothing, only
Your inference therefrom!

XI

My river runs to thee:
Blue sea, wilt welcome me?

My river waits reply.
Oh sea, look graciously!

I'll fetch thee brooks
From spotted nooks,—

Say, sea,
Take me!

XII

I cannot live with you,
It would be life,
And life is over there
Behind the shelf

The sexton keeps the key to,
Putting up
Our life, his porcelain,
Like a cup

Discarded of the housewife,
Quaint or broken;
A newer Sèvres pleases,
Old ones crack.

I could not die with you,
For one must wait
To shut the other's gaze down,—
You could not.

And I, could I stand by
And see you freeze,
Without my right of frost,
Death's privilege?

Nor could I rise with you,
Because your face
Would put out Jesus's,
That new grace

Glow plain and foreign
On my homesick eye,
Except that you, than he
Shone closer by.

They'd judge us—how?
For you served Heaven, you know,
Or sought to;
I could not,

Because you saturated sight,
And I had no more eyes
For sordid excellence
As Paradise.

And were you lost, I would be,
Though my name
Rang loudest
On the heavenly fame.

And were you saved,
And I condemned to be
Where you were not,
That self were hell to me.

So we must keep apart,
You there, I here,
With just the door ajar
That oceans are,
And prayer,
And that pale sustenance,
Despair!

XIII

There came a day at summer's full
Entirely for me;
I thought that such were for the saints,
Where revelations be.

The sun, as common, went abroad,
The flowers, accustomed, blew,
As if no sail the solstice passed
That maketh all things new.

The time was scarce profaned by speech;
The symbol of a word
Was needless, as at sacrament
The wardrobe of our Lord.

Each was to each the sealed church,
Permitted to commune this time,
Lest we too awkward show
At supper of the Lamb.

The hours slid fast, as hours will,
Clutched tight by greedy hands;
So faces on two decks look back,
Bound to opposing lands.

And so, when all the time had failed,
Without external sound,
Each bound the other's crucifix,
We gave no other bond.

Sufficient troth that we shall rise—
Deposed, at length, the grave—
To that new marriage, justified
Through Calvaries of Love!

XIV

I'm ceded, I've stopped being theirs;
The name they dropped upon my face
With water, in the country church,
Is finished using now,

And they can put it with my dolls,
My childhood, and the string of spools
I've finished threading too.

Baptized before without the choice,
But this time consciously, of grace
Unto supremest name,
Called to my full, the crescent dropped,
Existence's whole arc filled up
With one small diadem.

My second rank, too small the first,
Crowned, crowing on my father's breast,
A half unconscious queen;
But this time, adequate, erect,
With will to choose or to reject,
And I choose—just a throne.

XV

'T was a long parting, but the time
For interview had come;
Before the judgment-seat of God,
The last and second time

These fleshless lovers met,
A heaven in a gaze,
A heaven of heavens, the privilege
Of one another's eyes.

No lifetime set on them,
Apparelled as the new
Unborn, except they had beheld,
Born everlasting now.

Was bridal e'er like this?
A paradise, the host,
And cherubim and seraphim
The most familiar guest.

XVI

I'm wife; I've finished that,
That other state;
I'm Czar, I'm woman now:
It's safer so.

How odd the girl's life looks
Behind this soft eclipse!
I think that earth seems so
To those in heaven now.

This being comfort, then
That other kind was pain;
But why compare?
I'm wife! stop there!

XVII

She rose to his requirement, dropped
The playthings of her life
To take the honorable work
Of woman and of wife.

If aught she missed in her new day
Of amplitude, or awe,
Or first prospective, or the gold
In using wore away,

It lay unmentioned, as the sea
Develops! pearl and weed,

But only to himself is known
The fathoms they abide.

XVIII

Come slowly, Eden!
Lips unused to thee,
Bashful, sip thy jasmines,
As the fainting bee,

Reaching late his flower,
Round her chamber hums,
Counts his nectars—enters,
And is lost in balms!

XIX

Of all the souls that stand create
I have elected one.
When sense from spirit files away,
And subterfuge is done;

When that which is and that which was
Apart, intrinsic, stand,
And this brief tragedy of flesh
Is shifted like a sand;

When figures show their royal front
And mists are carved away,—
Behold the atom I preferred
To all the lists of clay!

XX

I have no life but this,
To lead it here;

Nor any death, but lest
Dispelled from there;

Nor tie to earths to come,
Nor action new,
Except through this extent,
The realm of you.

XXI

Your riches taught me poverty.
Myself a millionnaire
In little wealths,—as girls could boast,—
Till broad as Buenos Ayre,

You drifted your dominions
A different Peru;
And I esteemed all poverty,
For life's estate with you.

Of mines I little know, myself,
But just the names of gems,—
The colors of the commonest;
And scarce of diadems

So much that, did I meet the queen,
Her glory I should know:
But this must be a different wealth,
To miss it beggars so.

I'm sure 't is India all day
To those who look on you
Without a stint, without a blame,—
Might I but be the Jew!

I'm sure it is Golconda,
Beyond my power to deem,—
To have a smile for mine each day,
How better than a gem!

At least, it solaces to know
That there exists a gold,
Although I prove it just in time
Its distance to behold!

It's far, far treasure to surmise,
And estimate the pearl
That slipped my simple fingers through
While just a girl at school!

XXII

I gave myself to him,
And took himself for pay.
The solemn contract of a life
Was ratified this way.

The wealth might disappoint,
Myself a poorer prove
Than this great purchaser suspect,
The daily own of Love

Depreciate the vision;
But, till the merchant buy,
Still fable, in the isles of spice,
The subtle cargoes lie.

At least, 't is mutual risk,—
Some found it mutual gain;
Sweet debt of Life,—each night to owe,
Insolvent, every noon.

XXIII

"Going to him! Happy letter! Tell him—
Tell him the page I didn't write;
Tell him I only said the syntax,
And left the verb and the pronoun out.
Tell him just how the fingers hurried,
Then how they waded, slow, slow, slow;
And then you wished you had eyes in your pages,
So you could see what moved them so.

"Tell him it wasn't a practised writer,
You guessed, from the way the sentence toiled;
You could hear the bodice tug, behind you,
As if it held but the might of a child;
You almost pitied it, you, it worked so.
Tell him—No, you may quibble there,
For it would split his heart to know it,
And then you and I were silenter.

"Tell him night finished before we finished,
And the old clock kept neighing 'day!'
And you got sleepy and begged to be ended—
What could it hinder so, to say?
Tell him just how she sealed you, cautious,
But if he ask where you are hid
Until to-morrow,—happy letter!
Gesture, coquette, and shake your head!"

XXIV

The way I read a letter's this:
'T is first I lock the door,
And push it with my fingers next,
For transport it be sure.

And then I go the furthest off
To counteract a knock;
Then draw my little letter forth
And softly pick its lock.

Then, glancing narrow at the wall,
And narrow at the floor,
For firm conviction of a mouse
Not exorcised before,

Peruse how infinite I am
To—no one that you know!
And sigh for lack of heaven,—but not
The heaven the creeds bestow.

XXV

Wild nights! Wild nights!
Were I with thee,
Wild nights should be
Our luxury!

Futile the winds
To a heart in port,—
Done with the compass,
Done with the chart.

Rowing in Eden!
Ah! the sea!
Might I but moor
To-night in thee!

XXVI

The night was wide, and furnished scant
With but a single star,
That often as a cloud it met
Blew out itself for fear.

The wind pursued the little bush,
And drove away the leaves
November left; then clambered up
And fretted in the eaves.

No squirrel went abroad;
A dog's belated feet
Like intermittent plush were heard
Adown the empty street.

To feel if blinds be fast,
And closer to the fire
Her little rocking-chair to draw,
And shiver for the poor,

The housewife's gentle task.
"How pleasanter," said she
Unto the sofa opposite,
"The sleet than May—no thee!"

XXVII

Did the harebell loose her girdle
To the lover bee,
Would the bee the harebell hallow
Much as formerly?

Did the paradise, persuaded,
Yield her moat of pearl,
Would the Eden be an Eden,
Or the earl an earl?

XXVIII

A charm invests a face
Imperfectly beheld,—
The lady dare not lift her veil
For fear it be dispelled.

But peers beyond her mesh,
And wishes, and denies,—
Lest interview annul a want
That image satisfies.

XXIX

The rose did caper on her cheek,
Her bodice rose and fell,
Her pretty speech, like drunken men,
Did stagger pitiful.

Her fingers fumbled at her work,—
Her needle would not go;
What ailed so smart a little maid
It puzzled me to know,

Till opposite I spied a cheek
That bore another rose;
Just opposite, another speech
That like the drunkard goes;

A vest that, like the bodice, danced
To the immortal tune,—
Till those two troubled little clocks
Ticked softly into one.

XXX

In lands I never saw, they say,
Immortal Alps look down,
Whose bonnets touch the firmament,
Whose sandals touch the town,—

Meek at whose everlasting feet
A myriad daisies play.
Which, sir, are you, and which am I,
Upon an August day?

XXXI

The moon is distant from the sea,
And yet with amber hands
She leads him, docile as a boy,
Along appointed sands.

He never misses a degree;
Obedient to her eye,
He comes just so far toward the town,
Just so far goes away.

Oh, Signor, thine the amber hand,
And mine the distant sea,—
Obedient to the least command
Thine eyes impose on me.

XXXII

He put the belt around my life,—
I heard the buckle snap,
And turned away, imperial,
My lifetime folding up
Deliberate, as a duke would do
A kingdom's title-deed,—
Henceforth a dedicated sort,
A member of the cloud.

Yet not too far to come at call,
And do the little toils
That make the circuit of the rest,
And deal occasional smiles
To lives that stoop to notice mine
And kindly ask it in,—
Whose invitation, knew you not
For whom I must decline?

XXXIII

I held a jewel in my fingers
And went to sleep.
The day was warm, and winds were prosy;
I said: "'T will keep."

I woke and chid my honest fingers,—
The gem was gone;
And now an amethyst remembrance
Is all I own.

XXXIV

What if I say I shall not wait?
What if I burst the fleshly gate

And pass, escaped, to thee?
What if I file this mortal off,
See where it hurt me,—that's enough,—
And wade in liberty?

They cannot take us any more,—
Dungeons may call, and guns implore;
Unmeaning now, to me,
As laughter was an hour ago,
Or laces, or a travelling show,
Or who died yesterday!

XXXV

Proud of my broken heart since thou didst break it,
  Proud of the pain I did not feel till thee,
Proud of my night since thou with moons dost slake it,
  Not to partake thy passion, my humility.

XXXVI

My worthiness is all my doubt,
  His merit all my fear,
Contrasting which, my qualities
  Do lowlier appear;

Lest I should insufficient prove
  For his beloved need,
The chiefest apprehension
  Within my loving creed.

So I, the undivine abode
  Of his elect content,
Conform my soul as 't were a church
  Unto her sacrament.

XXXVII

Love is anterior to life,
Posterior to death,
Initial of creation, and
The exponent of breath.

XXXVIII

One blessing had I, than the rest
So larger to my eyes
That I stopped gauging, satisfied,
For this enchanted size.

It was the limit of my dream,
The focus of my prayer,—
A perfect, paralyzing bliss
Contented as despair.

I knew no more of want or cold,
Phantasms both become,
For this new value in the soul,
Supremest earthly sum.

The heaven below the heaven above
Obscured with ruddier hue.
Life's latitude leaned over-full;
The judgment perished, too.

Why joys so scantily disburse,
Why Paradise defer,
Why floods are served to us in bowls,—
I speculate no more.

XXXIX

When roses cease to bloom, dear,
  And violets are done,
When bumble-bees in solemn flight
  Have passed beyond the sun,

The hand that paused to gather
  Upon this summer's day
Will idle lie, in Auburn,—
  Then take my flower, pray!

XL

Summer for thee grant I may be
  When summer days are flown!
Thy music still when whippoorwill
  And oriole are done!

For thee to bloom, I'll skip the tomb
  And sow my blossoms o'er!
Pray gather me, Anemone,
  Thy flower forevermore!

XLI

Split the lark and you'll find the music,
  Bulb after bulb, in silver rolled,
Scantily dealt to the summer morning,
  Saved for your ear when lutes be old.

Loose the flood, you shall find it patent,
  Gush after gush, reserved for you;
Scarlet experiment! sceptic Thomas,
  Now, do you doubt that your bird was true?

XLII

To lose thee, sweeter than to gain
  All other hearts I knew.
'T is true the drought is destitute,
  But then I had the dew!

The Caspian has its realms of sand,
  Its other realm of sea;
Without the sterile perquisite
  No Caspian could be.

XLIII

Poor little heart!
  Did they forget thee?
Then dinna care! Then dinna care!

  Proud little heart!
  Did they forsake thee?
Be debonair! Be debonair!

  Frail little heart!
  I would not break thee:
Could'st credit me? Could'st credit me?

  Gay little heart!
  Like morning glory
Thou 'll wilted be; thou 'll wilted be!

XLIV

There is a word
Which bears a sword
  Can pierce an armed man.
It hurls its barbed syllables,—

At once is mute again.
But where it fell
The saved will tell
On patriotic day,
Some epauletted brother
Gave his breath away.
Wherever runs the breathless sun,
Wherever roams the day,
There is its noiseless onset,
There is its victory!
Behold the keenest marksman!
The most accomplished shot!
Time's sublimest target
Is a soul "forgot"!

XLV

I've got an arrow here;
Loving the hand that sent it,
I the dart revere.

Fell, they will say, in "skirmish"!
Vanquished, my soul will know,
By but a simple arrow
Sped by an archer's bow.

XLVI

He fumbles at your spirit
As players at the keys
Before they drop full music on;
He stuns you by degrees,

Prepares your brittle substance
For the ethereal blow,

By fainter hammers, further heard,
Then nearer, then so slow

Your breath has time to straighten,
Your brain to bubble cool,—
Deals one imperial thunderbolt
That scalps your naked soul.

XLVII

Heart, we will forget him!
You and I, to-night!
You may forget the warmth he gave,
I will forget the light.

When you have done, pray tell me,
That I my thoughts may dim;
Haste! lest while you're lagging,
I may remember him!

XLVIII

Father, I bring thee not myself,—
That were the little load;
I bring thee the imperial heart
I had not strength to hold.

The heart I cherished in my own
Till mine too heavy grew,
Yet strangest, heavier since it went,
Is it too large for you?

XLIX

We outgrow love like other things
And put it in the drawer,

Till it an antique fashion shows
Like costumes grandsires wore.

L

Not with a club the heart is broken,
Nor with a stone;
A whip, so small you could not see it,
I've known

To lash the magic creature
Till it fell,
Yet that whip's name too noble
Then to tell.

Magnanimous of bird
By boy descried,
To sing unto the stone
Of which it died.

LI

My friend must be a bird,
Because it flies!
Mortal my friend must be,
Because it dies!
Barbs has it, like a bee.
Ah, curious friend,
Thou puzzlest me!

LII

He touched me, so I live to know
That such a day, permitted so,
I groped upon his breast.

It was a boundless place to me,
And silenced, as the awful sea
    Puts minor streams to rest.

And now, I'm different from before,
As if I breathed superior air,
    Or brushed a royal gown;
My feet, too, that had wandered so,
My gypsy face transfigured now
    To tenderer renown.

LIII

Let me not mar that perfect dream
    By an auroral stain,
But so adjust my daily night
    That it will come again.

LIV

I live with him, I see his face;
    I go no more away
For visitor, or sundown;
    Death's single privacy,

The only one forestalling mine,
    And that by right that he
Presents a claim invisible,
    No wedlock granted me.

I live with him, I hear his voice,
    I stand alive to-day
To witness to the certainty
    Of immortality

Taught me by Time,—the lower way,
Conviction every day,—
That life like this is endless,
Be judgment what it may.

LV

I envy seas whereon he rides,
I envy spokes of wheels
Of chariots that him convey,
I envy speechless hills

That gaze upon his journey;
How easy all can see
What is forbidden utterly
As heaven, unto me!

I envy nests of sparrows
That dot his distant eaves,
The wealthy fly upon his pane,
The happy, happy leaves

That just abroad his window
Have summer's leave to be,
The earrings of Pizarro
Could not obtain for me.

I envy light that wakes him,
And bells that boldly ring
To tell him it is noon abroad,—
Myself his noon could bring,

Yet interdict my blossom
And abrogate my bee,
Lest noon in everlasting night
Drop Gabriel and me.

LVI

A solemn thing it was, I said,
  A woman white to be,
And wear, if God should count me fit,
  Her hallowed mystery.

A timid thing to drop a life
  Into the purple well,
Too plummetless that it come back
  Eternity until.

LVII

Title divine is mine
The Wife without
The Sign.
Acute degree
Conferred on me—
Empress of Calvary.
Royal all but the
Crown—
Betrothed, without the swoon
God gives us women
When two hold
Garnet to garnet,
Gold to gold—
Born—Bridalled—
Shrouded—
In a day
Tri-Victory—
  "My Husband"
Women say
Stroking the melody,
Is this the way?

PART FOUR

Time and Eternity

I

One dignity delays for all,
One mitred afternoon.
None can avoid this purple,
None evade this crown.

Coach it insures, and footmen,
Chamber and state and throng;
Bells, also, in the village,
As we ride grand along.

What dignified attendants,
What service when we pause!
How loyally at parting
Their hundred hats they raise!

How pomp surpassing ermine,
When simple you and I
Present our meek escutcheon,
And claim the rank to die!

II

Delayed till she had ceased to know,
Delayed till in its vest of snow
   Her loving bosom lay.
An hour behind the fleeting breath,
Later by just an hour than death,—
   Oh, lagging yesterday!

Could she have guessed that it would be;
Could but a crier of the glee
  Have climbed the distant hill;
Had not the bliss so slow a pace,—
Who knows but this surrendered face
  Were undefeated still?

Oh, if there may departing be
Any forgot by victory
  In her imperial round,
Show them this meek apparelled thing,
That could not stop to be a king,
  Doubtful if it be crowned!

III

Departed to the judgment,
A mighty afternoon;
Great clouds like ushers leaning,
Creation looking on.

The flesh surrendered, cancelled,
The bodiless begun;
Two worlds, like audiences, disperse
And leave the soul alone.

IV

Safe in their alabaster chambers,
Untouched by morning and untouched by noon,
Sleep the meek members of the resurrection,
Rafter of satin, and roof of stone.

Light laughs the breeze in her castle of sunshine;
Babbles the bee in a stolid ear;

Pipe the sweet birds in ignorant cadence,—
Ah, what sagacity perished here!

Grand go the years in the crescent above them;
Worlds scoop their arcs, and firmaments row,
Diadems drop and Doges surrender,
Soundless as dots on a disk of snow.

V

On this long storm the rainbow rose,
On this late morn the sun;
The clouds, like listless elephants,
Horizons straggled down.

The birds rose smiling in their nests,
The gales indeed were done;
Alas! how heedless were the eyes
On whom the summer shone!

The quiet nonchalance of death
No daybreak can bestir;
The slow archangel's syllables
Must awaken her.

VI

My cocoon tightens, colors tease,
I'm feeling for the air;
A dim capacity for wings
Degrades the dress I wear.

A power of butterfly must be
The aptitude to fly,
Meadows of majesty concedes
And easy sweeps of sky.

So I must baffle at the hint
And cipher at the sign,
And make much blunder, if at last
I take the clue divine.

VII

Exultation is the going
Of an inland soul to sea,—
Past the houses, past the headlands,
Into deep eternity!

Bred as we, among the mountains,
Can the sailor understand
The divine intoxication
Of the first league out from land?

VIII

Look back on time with kindly eyes,
He doubtless did his best;
How softly sinks his trembling sun
In human nature's west!

IX

A train went through a burial gate,
A bird broke forth and sang,
And trilled, and quivered, and shook his throat
Till all the churchyard rang;

And then adjusted his little notes,
And bowed and sang again.
Doubtless, he thought it meet of him
To say good-bye to men.

X

I died for beauty, but was scarce
Adjusted in the tomb,
When one who died for truth was lain
In an adjoining room.

He questioned softly why I failed?
"For beauty," I replied.
"And I for truth,—the two are one;
We brethren are," he said.

And so, as kinsmen met a night,
We talked between the rooms,
Until the moss had reached our lips,
And covered up our names.

XI

How many times these low feet staggered,
Only the soldered mouth can tell;
Try! can you stir the awful rivet?
Try! can you lift the hasps of steel?

Stroke the cool forehead, hot so often,
Lift, if you can, the listless hair;
Handle the adamantine fingers
Never a thimble more shall wear.

Buzz the dull flies on the chamber window;
Brave shines the sun through the freckled pane;
Fearless the cobweb swings from the ceiling—
Indolent housewife, in daisies lain!

XII

I like a look of agony,
Because I know it's true;
Men do not sham convulsion,
Nor simulate a throe.

The eyes glaze once, and that is death.
Impossible to feign
The beads upon the forehead
By homely anguish strung.

XIII

That short, potential stir
That each can make but once,
That bustle so illustrious
'T is almost consequence,

Is the *éclat* of death.
Oh, thou unknown renown
That not a beggar would accept,
Had he the power to spurn!

XIV

I went to thank her,
But she slept;
Her bed a funnelled stone,
With nosegays at the head and foot,
That travellers had thrown,

Who went to thank her;
But she slept.
'T was short to cross the sea

To look upon her like, alive,
But turning back 't was slow.

XV

I've seen a dying eye
Run round and round a room
In search of something, as it seemed,
Then cloudier become;
And then, obscure with fog,
And then be soldered down,
Without disclosing what it be,
'T were blessed to have seen.

XVI

The clouds their backs together laid,
The north begun to push,
The forests galloped till they fell,
The lightning skipped like mice;
The thunder crumbled like a stuff—
How good to be safe in tombs,
Where nature's temper cannot reach,
Nor vengeance ever comes!

XVII

I never saw a moor,
I never saw the sea;
Yet know I how the heather looks,
And what a wave must be.

I never spoke with God,
Nor visited in heaven;
Yet certain am I of the spot
As if the chart were given.

XVIII

God permits industrious angels
Afternoons to play.
I met one,—forgot my school-mates,
All, for him, straightaway.

God calls home the angels promptly
At the setting sun;
I missed mine. How dreary marbles,
After playing Crown!

XIX

To know just how he suffered would be dear;
To know if any human eyes were near
To whom he could entrust his wavering gaze,
Until it settled firm on Paradise.

To know if he was patient, part content,
Was dying as he thought, or different;
Was it a pleasant day to die,
And did the sunshine face his way?

What was his furthest mind, of home, or God,
Or what the distant say
At news that he ceased human nature
On such a day?

And wishes, had he any?
Just his sigh, accented,
Had been legible to me.
And was he confident until
Ill fluttered out in everlasting well?

And if he spoke, what name was best,
What first,
What one broke off with
At the drowsiest?

Was he afraid, or tranquil?
Might he know
How conscious consciousness could grow,
Till love that was, and love too blessed to be,
Meet—and the junction be Eternity?

XX

The last night that she lived,
It was a common night,
Except the dying; this to us
Made nature different.

We noticed smallest things,—
Things overlooked before,
By this great light upon our minds
Italicized, as 't were.

That others could exist
While she must finish quite,
A jealousy for her arose
So nearly infinite.

We waited while she passed;
It was a narrow time,
Too jostled were our souls to speak,
At length the notice came.

She mentioned, and forgot;
Then lightly as a reed

Bent to the water, shivered scarce,
Consented, and was dead.

And we, we placed the hair,
And drew the head erect;
And then an awful leisure was,
Our faith to regulate.

XXI

Not in this world to see his face
Sounds long, until I read the place
Where this is said to be
But just the primer to a life
Unopened, rare, upon the shelf,
Clasped yet to him and me.

And yet, my primer suits me so
I would not choose a book to know
Than that, be sweeter wise;
Might some one else so learned be,
And leave me just my A B C,
Himself could have the skies.

XXII

The bustle in a house
The morning after death
Is solemnest of industries
Enacted upon earth,—

The sweeping up the heart,
And putting love away
We shall not want to use again
Until eternity.

XXIII

I reason, earth is short,
And anguish absolute.
And many hurt;
But what of that?

I reason, we could die:
The best vitality
Cannot excel decay;
But what of that?

I reason that in heaven
Somehow, it will be even,
Some new equation given;
But what of that?

XXIV

Afraid? Of whom am I afraid?
Not death; for who is he?
The porter of my father's lodge
As much abasheth me.

Of life? 'T were odd I fear a thing
That comprehendeth me
In one or more existences
At Deity's decree.

Of resurrection? Is the east
Afraid to trust the morn
With her fastidious forehead?
As soon impeach my crown!

XXV

The sun kept setting, setting still;
No hue of afternoon
Upon the village I perceived,—
From house to house 't was noon.

The dusk kept dropping, dropping still;
No dew upon the grass,
But only on my forehead stopped,
And wandered in my face.

My feet kept drowsing, drowsing still,
My fingers were awake;
Yet why so little sound myself
Unto my seeming make?

How well I knew the light before!
I could not see it now.
'T is dying, I am doing; but
I'm not afraid to know.

XXVI

Two swimmers wrestled on the spar
Until the morning sun,
When one turned smiling to the land.
O God, the other one!

The stray ships passing spied a face
Upon the waters borne,
With eyes in death still begging raised,
And hands beseeching thrown.

XXVII

Because I could not stop for Death,
He kindly stopped for me;
The carriage held but just ourselves
And Immortality.

We slowly drove, he knew no haste,
And I had put away
My labor, and my leisure too,
For his civility.

We passed the school where children played
At wrestling in a ring;
We passed the fields of gazing grain,
We passed the setting sun.

We paused before a house that seemed
A swelling of the ground;
The roof was scarcely visible,
The cornice but a mound.

Since then 't is centuries; but each
Feels shorter than the day
I first surmised the horses' heads
Were toward eternity.

XXVIII

She went as quiet as the dew
From a familiar flower.
Not like the dew did she return
At the accustomed hour!

She dropped as softly as a star
From out my summer's eve;

Less skillful than Leverrier
It's sorer to believe!

XXIX

At last to be identified!
At last, the lamps upon thy side,
The rest of life to see!
Past midnight, past the morning star!
Past sunrise! Ah! what leagues there are
Between our feet and day!

XXX

Except to heaven, she is nought;
Except for angels, lone;
Except to some wide-wandering bee,
A flower superfluous blown;

Except for winds, provincial;
Except by butterflies,
Unnoticed as a single dew
That on the acre lies.

The smallest housewife in the grass,
Yet take her from the lawn,
And somebody has lost the face
That made existence home!

XXXI

Death is a dialogue between
The spirit and the dust.
"Dissolve," says Death. The Spirit, "Sir,
I have another trust."

Death doubts it, argues from the ground.
The Spirit turns away,
Just laying off, for evidence,
An overcoat of clay.

XXXII

It was too late for man,
But early yet for God;
Creation impotent to help,
But prayer remained our side.

How excellent the heaven,
When earth cannot be had;
How hospitable, then, the face
Of our old neighbor, God!

XXXIII

When I was small, a woman died.
To-day her only boy
Went up from the Potomac,
His face all victory,

To look at her; how slowly
The seasons must have turned
Till bullets clipped an angle,
And he passed quickly round!

If pride shall be in Paradise
I never can decide;
Of their imperial conduct,
No person testified.

But proud in apparition,
That woman and her boy

Pass back and forth before my brain,
As ever in the sky.

XXXIV

The daisy follows soft the sun,
And when his golden walk is done,
Sits shyly at his feet.
He, waking, finds the flower near.
"Wherefore, marauder, art thou here?"
"Because, sir, love is sweet!"

We are the flower, Thou the sun!
Forgive us, if as days decline,
We nearer steal to Thee,—
Enamoured of the parting west,
The peace, the flight, the amethyst,
Night's possibility!

XXXV

No rack can torture me,
My soul's at liberty.
Behind this mortal bone
There knits a bolder one

You cannot prick with saw,
Nor rend with scimitar.
Two bodies therefore be;
Bind one, and one will flee.

The eagle of his nest
No easier divest
And gain the sky,
Than mayest thou,

Except thyself may be
Thine enemy;
Captivity is consciousness,
So's liberty.

XXXVI

I lost a world the other day.
Has anybody found?
You'll know it by the row of stars
Around its forehead bound.

A rich man might not notice it;
Yet to my frugal eye
Of more esteem than ducats.
Oh, find it, sir, for me!

XXXVII

If I shouldn't be alive
When the robins come,
Give the one in red cravat
A memorial crumb.

If I couldn't thank you,
Being just asleep,
You will know I'm trying
With my granite lip!

XXXVIII

Sleep is supposed to be,
By souls of sanity,
The shutting of the eye.

Sleep is the station grand
Down which on either hand
The hosts of witness stand!

Morn is supposed to be,
By people of degree,
The breaking of the day.

Morning has not occurred!
That shall aurora be
East of eternity;

One with the banner gay,
One in the red array,—
That is the break of day.

XXXIX

I shall know why, when time is over,
And I have ceased to wonder why;
Christ will explain each separate anguish
In the fair schoolroom of the sky.

He will tell me what Peter promised,
And I, for wonder at his woe,
I shall forget the drop of anguish
That scalds me now, that scalds me now.

XL

I never lost as much but twice,
And that was in the sod;
Twice have I stood a beggar
Before the door of God!

Angels, twice descending,
Reimbursed my store.
Burglar, banker, father,
I am poor once more!

XLI

Let down the bars, O Death!
The tired flocks come in
Whose bleating ceases to repeat,
Whose wandering is done.

Thine is the stillest night,
Thine the securest fold;
Too near thou art for seeking thee,
Too tender to be told.

XLII

Going to heaven!
I don't know when,
Pray do not ask me how,—
Indeed, I'm too astonished
To think of answering you!
Going to heaven!—
How dim it sounds!
And yet it will be done
As sure as flocks go home at night
Unto the shepherd's arm!

Perhaps you're going too!
Who knows?
If you should get there first,
Save just a little place for me
Close to the two I lost!

The smallest "robe" will fit me,
And just a bit of "crown";
For you know we do not mind our dress
When we are going home.

I'm glad I don't believe it,
For it would stop my breath,
And I'd like to look a little more
At such a curious earth!
I am glad they did believe it
Whom I have never found
Since the mighty autumn afternoon
I left them in the ground.

XLIII

At least to pray is left, is left,
O Jesus! in the air
I know not which thy chamber is,—
I'm knocking everywhere.

Thou stirrest earthquake in the South,
And maelstrom in the sea;
Say, Jesus Christ of Nazareth,
Hast thou no arm for me?

XLIV

Step lightly on this narrow spot!
The broadest land that grows
Is not so ample as the breast
These emerald seams enclose.

Step lofty; for this name is told
As far as cannon dwell,
Or flag subsist, or fame export
Her deathless syllable.

XLV

Morns like these we parted;
Noons like these she rose,
Fluttering first, then firmer,
To her fair repose.

Never did she lisp it,
And 't was not for me;
She was mute from transport,
I, from agony!

Till the evening, nearing,
One the shutters drew—
Quick! a sharper rustling!
And this linnet flew!

XLVI

A death-blow is a life-blow to some
Who, till they died, did not alive become;
Who, had they lived, had died, but when
They died, vitality begun.

XLVII

I read my sentence steadily,
Reviewed it with my eyes,
To see that I made no mistake
In its extremest clause,—

The date, and manner of the shame;
And then the pious form
That "God have mercy" on the soul
The jury voted him.

I made my soul familiar
With her extremity,
That at the last it should not be
A novel agony,

But she and Death, acquainted,
Meet tranquilly as friends,
Salute and pass without a hint—
And there the matter ends.

XLVIII

I have not told my garden yet,
Lest that should conquer me;
I have not quite the strength now
To break it to the bee.

I will not name it in the street,
For shops would stare, that I,
So shy, so very ignorant,
Should have the face to die.

The hillsides must not know it,
Where I have rambled so,
Nor tell the loving forests
The day that I shall go,

Nor lisp it at the table,
Nor heedless by the way
Hint that within the riddle
One will walk to-day!

XLIX

They dropped like flakes, they dropped like stars,
Like petals from a rose,

When suddenly across the June
  A wind with fingers goes.

They perished in the seamless grass,—
  No eye could find the place;
But God on his repealless list
  Can summon every face.

L

The only ghost I ever saw
Was dressed in mechlin,—so;
He wore no sandal on his foot,
And stepped like flakes of snow.
His gait was soundless, like the bird,
But rapid, like the roe;
His fashions quaint, mosaic,
Or, haply, mistletoe.

His conversation seldom,
His laughter like the breeze
That dies away in dimples
Among the pensive trees.
Our interview was transient,—
Of me, himself was shy;
And God forbid I look behind
Since that appalling day!

LI

Some, too fragile for winter winds,
The thoughtful grave encloses,—
Tenderly tucking them in from frost
Before their feet are cold.

Never the treasures in her nest
The cautious grave exposes,
Building where schoolboy dare not look
And sportsman is not bold.

This covert have all the children
Early aged, and often cold,—
Sparrows unnoticed by the Father;
Lambs for whom time had not a fold.

LII

As by the dead we love to sit,
Become so wondrous dear,
As for the lost we grapple,
Though all the rest are here,—

In broken mathematics
We estimate our prize,
Vast, in its fading ratio,
To our penurious eyes!

LIII

Death sets a thing significant
The eye had hurried by,
Except a perished creature
Entreat us tenderly

To ponder little workmanships
In crayon or in wool,
With "This was last her fingers did,"
Industrious until

The thimble weighed too heavy,
The stitches stopped themselves,
And then 't was put among the dust
Upon the closet shelves.

A book I have, a friend gave,
Whose pencil, here and there,
Had notched the place that pleased him.—
At rest his fingers are.

Now, when I read, I read not,
For interrupting tears
Obliterate the etchings
Too costly for repairs.

LIV

I went to heaven,—
'T was a small town,
Lit with a ruby,
Lathed with down.
Stiller than the fields
At the full dew,
Beautiful as pictures
No man drew.
People like the moth,
Of mechlin, frames,
Duties of gossamer,
And eider names.
Almost contented
I could be
'Mong such unique
Society.

LV

Their height in heaven comforts not,
Their glory nought to me;
'T was best imperfect, as it was;
I'm finite, I can't see.

The house of supposition,
The glimmering frontier
That skirts the acres of perhaps,
To me shows insecure.

The wealth I had contented me;
If 't was a meaner size,
Then I had counted it until
It pleased my narrow eyes

Better than larger values,
However true their show;
This timid life of evidence
Keeps pleading, "I don't know."

LVI

There is a shame of nobleness
Confronting sudden pelf,—
A finer shame of ecstasy
Convicted of itself.

A best disgrace a brave man feels,
Acknowledged of the brave,—
One more "Ye Blessed" to be told;
But this involves the grave.

LVII

A triumph may be of several kinds.
There's triumph in the room
When that old imperator, Death,
By faith is overcome.

There's triumph of the finer mind
When truth, affronted long,
Advances calm to her supreme,
Her God her only throng.

A triumph when temptation's bribe
Is slowly handed back,
One eye upon the heaven renounced
And one upon the rack.

Severer triumph, by himself
Experienced, who can pass
Acquitted from that naked bar,
Jehovah's countenance!

LVIII

Pompless no life can pass away;
　The lowliest career
To the same pageant wends its way
　As that exalted here.
How cordial is the mystery!
　The hospitable pall
A "this way" beckons spaciously,—
　A miracle for all!

LIX

I noticed people disappeared,
When but a little child,—
Supposed they visited remote,
Or settled regions wild.

Now know I they both visited
And settled regions wild,
But did because they died,—a fact
Withheld the little child!

LX

I had no cause to be awake,
My best was gone to sleep,
And morn a new politeness took
And failed to wake them up,

But called the others clear,
And passed their curtains by.
Sweet morning, when I over-sleep,
Knock, recollect, for me!

I looked at sunrise once,
And then I looked at them,
And wishfulness in me arose
For circumstance the same.

'T was such an ample peace,
It could not hold a sigh,—
'T was Sabbath with the bells divorced,
'T was sunset all the day.

So choosing but a gown
And taking but a prayer,

The only raiment I should need,
I struggled, and was there.

LXI

If anybody's friend be dead,
It's sharpest of the theme
The thinking how they walked alive,
At such and such a time.

Their costume, of a Sunday,
Some manner of the hair,—
A prank nobody knew but them,
Lost, in the sepulchre.

How warm they were on such a day:
You almost feel the date,
So short way off it seems; and now,
They're centuries from that.

How pleased they were at what you said;
You try to touch the smile,
And dip your fingers in the frost:
When was it, can you tell,

You asked the company to tea,
Acquaintance, just a few,
And chatted close with this grand thing
That don't remember you?

Past bows and invitations,
Past interview, and vow,
Past what ourselves can estimate,—
That makes the quick of woe!

LXII

Our journey had advanced;
Our feet were almost come
To that odd fork in Being's road,
Eternity by term.

Our pace took sudden awe,
Our feet reluctant led.
Before were cities, but between,
The forest of the dead.

Retreat was out of hope,—
Behind, a sealed route,
Eternity's white flag before,
And God at every gate.

LXIII

Ample make this bed.
Make this bed with awe;
In it wait till judgment break
Excellent and fair.

Be its mattress straight,
Be its pillow round;
Let no sunrise' yellow noise
Interrupt this ground.

LXIV

On such a night, or such a night,
Would anybody care
If such a little figure
Slipped quiet from its chair,

So quiet, oh, how quiet!
That nobody might know
But that the little figure
Rocked softer, to and fro?

On such a dawn, or such a dawn,
Would anybody sigh
That such a little figure
Too sound asleep did lie

For chanticleer to wake it,—
Or stirring house below,
Or giddy bird in orchard,
Or early task to do?

There was a little figure plump
For every little knoll,
Busy needles, and spools of thread,
And trudging feet from school.

Playmates, and holidays, and nuts,
And visions vast and small.
Strange that the feet so precious charged
Should reach so small a goal!

LXV

Essential oils are wrung:
The attar from the rose
Is not expressed by suns alone,
It is the gift of screws.

The general rose decays;
But this, in lady's drawer,
Makes summer when the lady lies
In ceaseless rosemary.

LXVI

I lived on dread; to those who know
The stimulus there is
In danger, other impetus
Is numb and vital-less.

As 't were a spur upon the soul,
A fear will urge it where
To go without the spectre's aid
Were challenging despair.

LXVII

If I should die,
And you should live,
And time should gurgle on,
And morn should beam,
And noon should burn,
As it has usual done;
If birds should build as early,
And bees as bustling go,—
One might depart at option
From enterprise below!
'T is sweet to know that stocks will stand
When we with daisies lie,
That commerce will continue,
And trades as briskly fly.
It makes the parting tranquil
And keeps the soul serene,
That gentlemen so sprightly
Conduct the pleasing scene!

LXVIII

Her final summer was it,
And yet we guessed it not;
If tenderer industriousness
Pervaded her, we thought

A further force of life
Developed from within,—
When Death lit all the shortness up,
And made the hurry plain.

We wondered at our blindness,—
When nothing was to see
But her Carrara guide-post,—
At our stupidity,

When, duller than our dullness,
The busy darling lay,
So busy was she, finishing,
So leisurely were we!

LXIX

One need not be a chamber to be haunted,
One need not be a house;
The brain has corridors surpassing
Material place.

Far safer, of a midnight meeting
External ghost,
Than an interior confronting
That whiter host.

Far safer through an Abbey gallop,
The stones achase,

Than, moonless, one's own self encounter
In lonesome place.

Ourself, behind ourself concealed,
Should startle most;
Assassin, hid in our apartment,
Be horror's least.

The prudent carries a revolver,
He bolts the door,
O'erlooking a superior spectre
More near.

LXX

She died,—this was the way she died;
And when her breath was done,
Took up her simple wardrobe
And started for the sun.

Her little figure at the gate
The angels must have spied,
Since I could never find her
Upon the mortal side.

LXXI

Wait till the majesty of Death
Invests so mean a brow!
Almost a powdered footman
Might dare to touch it now!

Wait till in everlasting robes
This democrat is dressed,
Then prate about "preferment"
And "station" and the rest!

Around this quiet courtier
Obsequious angels wait!
Full royal is his retinue,
Full purple is his state!

A lord might dare to lift the hat
To such a modest clay,
Since that my Lord, "the Lord of lords"
Receives unblushingly!

LXXII

Went up a year this evening!
I recollect it well!
Amid no bells nor bravos
The bystanders will tell!
Cheerful, as to the village,
Tranquil, as to repose,
Chastened, as to the chapel,
This humble tourist rose.
Did not talk of returning,
Alluded to no time
When, were the gales propitious,
We might look for him;
Was grateful for the roses
In life's diverse bouquet,
Talked softly of new species
To pick another day.
Beguiling thus the wonder,
The wondrous nearer drew;
Hands bustled at the moorings—
The crowd respectful grew.
Ascended from our vision
To countenances new!
A difference, a daisy,
Is all the rest I knew!

LXXIII

Taken from men this morning,
Carried by men to-day,
Met by the gods with banners
Who marshalled her away.

One little maid from playmates,
One little mind from school,—
There must be guests in Eden;
All the rooms are full.

Far as the east from even,
Dim as the border star,—
Courtiers quaint, in kingdoms,
Our departed are.

LXXIV

What inn is this
Where for the night
Peculiar traveller comes?
Who is the landlord?
Where the maids?
Behold, what curious rooms!
No ruddy fires on the hearth,
No brimming tankards flow.
Necromancer, landlord,
Who are these below?

LXXV

It was not death, for I stood up,
And all the dead lie down;
It was not night, for all the bells
Put out their tongues, for noon.

It was not frost, for on my flesh
I felt siroccos crawl,—
Nor fire, for just my marble feet
Could keep a chancel cool.

And yet it tasted like them all;
The figures I have seen
Set orderly, for burial,
Reminded me of mine,

As if my life were shaven
And fitted to a frame,
And could not breathe without a key;
And 't was like midnight, some,

When everything that ticked has stopped,
And space stares, all around,
Or grisly frosts, first autumn morns,
Repeal the beating ground.

But most like chaos,—stopless, cool,—
Without a chance or spar,
Or even a report of land
To justify despair.

LXXVI

I should not dare to leave my friend,
Because—because if he should die
While I was gone, and I—too late—
Should reach the heart that wanted me;

If I should disappoint the eyes
That hunted, hunted so, to see,
And could not bear to shut until
They "noticed" me—they noticed me;

If I should stab the patient faith
So sure I'd come—so sure I'd come,
It listening, listening, went to sleep
Telling my tardy name,—

My heart would wish it broke before,
Since breaking then, since breaking then,
Were useless as next morning's sun,
Where midnight frosts had lain!

LXXVII

Great streets of silence led away
To neighborhoods of pause;
Here was no notice, no dissent,
No universe, no laws.

By clocks 't was morning, and for night
The bells at distance called;
But epoch had no basis here,
For period exhaled.

LXXVIII

A throe upon the features
A hurry in the breath,
An ecstasy of parting
Denominated "Death,"—

An anguish at the mention,
Which, when to patience grown,
I've known permission given
To rejoin its own.

LXXIX

Of tribulation these are they
Denoted by the white;
The spangled gowns, a lesser rank
Of victors designate.

All these did conquer; but the ones
Who overcame most times
Wear nothing commoner than snow,
No ornament but palms.

Surrender is a sort unknown
On this superior soil;
Defeat, an outgrown anguish,
Remembered as the mile

Our panting ankle barely gained
When night devoured the road;
But we stood whispering in the house,
And all we said was "Saved!"

LXXX

I think just how my shape will rise
When I shall be forgiven,
Till hair and eyes and timid head
Are out of sight, in heaven.

I think just how my lips will weigh
With shapeless, quivering prayer
That you, so late, consider me,
The sparrow of your care.

I mind me that of anguish sent,
Some drifts were moved away

Before my simple bosom broke,—
And why not this, if they?

And so, until delirious borne
I con that thing,—"forgiven,"—
Till with long fright and longer trust
I drop my heart, unshriven!

LXXXI

After a hundred years
Nobody knows the place,—
Agony, that enacted there,
Motionless as peace.

Weeds triumphant ranged,
Strangers strolled and spelled
At the lone orthography
Of the elder dead.

Winds of summer fields
Recollect the way,—
Instinct picking up the key
Dropped by memory.

LXXXII

Lay this laurel on the one
Too intrinsic for renown.
Laurel! veil your deathless tree,—
Him you chasten, that is he!

LXXXIII

This world is not conclusion;
A sequel stands beyond,

Invisible, as music,
  But positive, as sound.
It beckons and it baffles;
  Philosophies don't know,
And through a riddle, at the last,
  Sagacity must go.
To guess it puzzles scholars;
  To gain it, men have shown
Contempt of generations,
  And crucifixion known.

LXXXIV

We learn in the retreating
  How vast an one
Was recently among us.
  A perished sun

Endears in the departure
  How doubly more
Than all the golden presence
  It was before!

LXXXV

They say that "time assuages,"—
  Time never did assuage;
An actual suffering strengthens,
  As sinews do, with age.

Time is a test of trouble,
  But not a remedy.
If such it prove, it prove too
  There was no malady.

LXXXVI

We cover thee, sweet face.
Not that we tire of thee,
But that thyself fatigue of us;
Remember, as thou flee,
We follow thee until
Thou notice us no more,
And then, reluctant, turn away
To con thee o'er and o'er,
And blame the scanty love
We were content to show,
Augmented, sweet, a hundred fold
If thou would'st take it now.

LXXXVII

That is solemn we have ended,—
Be it but a play,
Or a glee among the garrets,
Or a holiday,

Or a leaving home; or later,
Parting with a world
We have understood, for better
Still it be unfurled.

LXXXVIII

The stimulus, beyond the grave
His countenance to see,
Supports me like imperial drams
Afforded royally.

LXXXIX

Given in marriage unto thee,
Oh, thou celestial host!
Bride of the Father and the Son,
Bride of the Holy Ghost!

Other betrothal shall dissolve,
Wedlock of will decay;
Only the keeper of this seal
Conquers mortality.

XC

That such have died enables us
The tranquiller to die;
That such have lived, certificate
For immortality.

XCI

They won't frown always,—some sweet day
When I forget to tease,
They'll recollect how cold I looked,
And how I just said "please."

Then they will hasten to the door
To call the little child,
Who cannot thank them, for the ice
That on her lisping piled.

XCII

'T is an honorable thought,
And makes one lift one's hat,

As one encountered gentlefolk
  Upon a daily street,

That we've immortal place,
  Though pyramids decay,
And kingdoms, like the orchard,
  Flit russetly away.

XCIII

The distance that the dead have gone
  Does not at first appear;
Their coming back seems possible
  For many an ardent year.

And then, that we have followed them
  We more than half suspect,
So intimate have we become
  With their dear retrospect.

XCIV

How dare the robins sing,
  When men and women hear
Who since they went to their account
  Have settled with the year!—
Paid all that life had earned
  In one consummate bill,
And now, what life or death can do
  Is immaterial.
Insulting is the sun
  To him whose mortal light,
Beguiled of immortality,
  Bequeaths him to the night.
In deference to him
  Extinct be every hum,

Whose garden wrestles with the dew,
  At daybreak overcome!

XCV

Death is like the insect
  Menacing the tree,
Competent to kill it,
  But decoyed may be.

Bait it with the balsam,
  Seek it with the knife,
Baffle, if it cost you
  Everything in life.

Then, if it have burrowed
  Out of reach of skill,
Ring the tree and leave it,—
  'T is the vermin's will.

XCVI

'T is sunrise, little maid, hast thou
  No station in the day?
'T was not thy wont to hinder so,—
  Retrieve thine industry.

'T is noon, my little maid, alas!
  And art thou sleeping yet?
The lily waiting to be wed,
  The bee, dost thou forget?

My little maid, 't is night; alas,
  That night should be to thee
Instead of morning! Hadst thou broached
  Thy little plan to me,

Dissuade thee if I could not, sweet,
  I might have aided thee.

XCVII

Each that we lose takes part of us;
A crescent still abides,
Which like the moon, some turbid night,
Is summoned by the tides.

XCVIII

Not any higher stands the grave
  For heroes than for men;
Not any nearer for the child
  Than numb three-score and ten.

This latest leisure equal lulls
  The beggar and his queen;
Propitiate this democrat
  By summer's gracious mien.

XCIX

As far from pity as complaint,
  As cool to speech as stone,
As numb to revelation
  As if my trade were bone.

As far from time as history,
  As near yourself to-day
As children to the rainbow's scarf,
  Or sunset's yellow play

To eyelids in the sepulchre.
  How still the dancer lies,

While color's revelations break,
And blaze the butterflies!

C

'T is whiter than an Indian pipe,
'T is dimmer than a lace;
No stature has it, like a fog,
When you approach the place.

Not any voice denotes it here,
Or intimates it there;
A spirit, how doth it accost?
What customs hath the air?

This limitless hyperbole
Each one of us shall be;
'T is drama, if (hypothesis)
It be not tragedy!

CI

She laid her docile crescent down,
And this mechanic stone
Still states, to dates that have forgot,
The news that she is gone.

So constant to its stolid trust,
The shaft that never knew,
It shames the constancy that fled
Before its emblem flew.

CII

Bless God, he went as soldiers,
His musket on his breast;

Grant, God, he charge the bravest
  Of all the martial blessed.

Please God, might I behold him
  In epauletted white,
I should not fear the foe then,
  I should not fear the fight.

CIII

Immortal is an ample word
  When what we need is by,
But when it leaves us for a time,
  'T is a necessity.

Of heaven above the firmest proof
  We fundamental know,
Except for its marauding hand,
  It had been heaven below.

CIV

Where every bird is bold to go,
  And bees abashless play,
The foreigner before he knocks
  Must thrust the tears away.

CV

The grave my little cottage is,
  Where, keeping house for thee,
I make my parlor orderly,
  And lay the marble tea,

For two divided, briefly,
  A cycle, it may be,

Till everlasting life unite
  In strong society.

CVI

This was in the white of the year,
  That was in the green,
Drifts were as difficult then to think
  As daisies now to be seen.

Looking back is best that is left,
  Or if it be before,
Retrospection is prospect's half,
  Sometimes almost more.

CVII

Sweet hours have perished here;
  This is a mighty room;
Within its precincts hopes have played,—
  Now shadows in the tomb.

CVIII

Me! Come! My dazzled face
  In such a shining place!

Me! Hear! My foreign ear
  The sounds of welcome near!

The saints shall meet
  Our bashful feet.

My holiday shall be
  That they remember me;

My paradise, the fame
That they pronounce my name.

CIX

From us she wandered now a year,
Her tarrying unknown;
If wilderness prevent her feet,
Or that ethereal zone

No eye hath seen and lived,
We ignorant must be.
We only know what time of year
We took the mystery.

CX

I wish I knew that woman's name,
So, when she comes this way,
To hold my life, and hold my ears,
For fear I hear her say

She's "sorry I am dead," again,
Just when the grave and I
Have sobbed ourselves almost to sleep,—
Our only lullaby.

CXI

Bereaved of all, I went abroad,
No less bereaved to be
Upon a new peninsula,—
The grave preceded me,

Obtained my lodgings ere myself,
And when I sought my bed,

The grave it was, reposed upon
   The pillow for my head.

I waked, to find it first awake,
   I rose,—it followed me;
I tried to drop it in the crowd,
   To lose it in the sea,

In cups of artificial drowse
   To sleep its shape away,—
The grave was finished, but the spade
   Remained in memory.

CXII

I felt a funeral in my brain,
   And mourners, to and fro,
Kept treading, treading, till it seemed
   That sense was breaking through.

And when they all were seated,
   A service like a drum
Kept beating, beating, till I thought
   My mind was going numb.

And then I heard them lift a box,
   And creak across my soul
With those same boots of lead, again.
   Then space began to toll

As all the heavens were a bell,
   And Being but an ear,
And I and silence some strange race,
   Wrecked, solitary, here.

CXIII

I meant to find her when I came;
   Death had the same design;
But the success was his, it seems,
   And the discomfit mine.

I meant to tell her how I longed
   For just this single time;
But Death had told her so the first,
   And she had hearkened him.

To wander now is my abode;
   To rest,—to rest would be
A privilege of hurricane
   To memory and me.

CXIV

I sing to use the waiting,
   My bonnet but to tie,
And shut the door unto my house;
   No more to do have I,

Till, his best step approaching,
   We journey to the day,
And tell each other how we sang
   To keep the dark away.

CXV

A sickness of this world it most occasions
   When best men die;
A wishfulness their far condition
   To occupy.

A chief indifference, as foreign
  A world must be
Themselves forsake contented,
  For Deity.

CXVI

Superfluous were the sun
  When excellence is dead;
He were superfluous every day,
  For every day is said

That syllable whose faith
  Just saves it from despair,
And whose "I'll meet you" hesitates—
  If love inquire, "Where?"

Upon his dateless fame
  Our periods may lie,
As stars that drop anonymous
  From an abundant sky.

CXVII

So proud she was to die
  It made us all ashamed
That what we cherished, so unknown
  To her desire seemed.

So satisfied to go
  Where none of us should be,
Immediately, that anguish stooped
  Almost to jealousy.

CXVIII

Tie the strings to my life, my Lord,
  Then I am ready to go!
Just a look at the horses—
  Rapid! That will do!

Put me in on the firmest side,
  So I shall never fall;
For we must ride to the Judgment,
  And it's partly down hill.

But never I mind the bridges,
  And never I mind the sea;
Held fast in everlasting race
  By my own choice and thee.

Good-bye to the life I used to live,
  And the world I used to know;
And kiss the hills for me, just once;
  Now I am ready to go!

CXIX

The dying need but little, dear,—
  A glass of water's all,
A flower's unobtrusive face
  To punctuate the wall,

A fan, perhaps, a friend's regret,
  And certainly that one
No color in the rainbow
  Perceives when you are gone.

CXX

There's something quieter than sleep
Within this inner room!
It wears a sprig upon its breast,
And will not tell its name.

Some touch it and some kiss it,
Some chafe its idle hand;
It has a simple gravity
I do not understand!

While simple-hearted neighbors
Chat of the "early dead,"
We, prone to periphrasis,
Remark that birds have fled!

CXXI

The soul should always stand ajar,
That if the heaven inquire,
He will not be obliged to wait,
Or shy of troubling her.

Depart, before the host has slid
The bolt upon the door,
To seek for the accomplished guest,—
Her visitor no more.

CXXII

Three weeks passed since I had seen her,—
Some disease had vexed;
'T was with text and village singing
I beheld her next,

And a company—our pleasure
  To discourse alone;
Gracious now to me as any,
  Gracious unto none.

Borne, without dissent of either,
  To the parish night;
Of the separated people
  Which are out of sight?

CXXIII

I breathed enough to learn the trick,
  And now, removed from air,
I simulate the breath so well,
  That one, to be quite sure

The lungs are stirless, must descend
  Among the cunning cells,
And touch the pantomime himself.
  How cool the bellows feels!

CXXIV

I wonder if the sepulchre
  Is not a lonesome way,
When men and boys, and larks and June
  Go down the fields to hay!

CXXV

If tolling bell I ask the cause.
  "A soul has gone to God,"
I'm answered in a lonesome tone;
  Is heaven then so sad?

That bells should joyful ring to tell
A soul had gone to heaven,
Would seem to me the proper way
A good news should be given.

CXXVI

If I may have it when it's dead
I will contented be;
If just as soon as breath is out
It shall belong to me,

Until they lock it in the grave,
'T is bliss I cannot weigh,
For though they lock thee in the grave,
Myself can hold the key.

Think of it, lover! I and thee
Permitted face to face to be;
After a life, a death we'll say,—
For death was that, and this is thee.

CXXVII

Before the ice is in the pools,
Before the skaters go,
Or any cheek at nightfall
Is tarnished by the snow,

Before the fields have finished,
Before the Christmas tree,
Wonder upon wonder
Will arrive to me!

What we touch the hems of
On a summer's day;

What is only walking
  Just a bridge away;

That which sings so, speaks so,
  When there's no one here,—
Will the frock I wept in
  Answer me to wear?

CXXVIII

I heard a fly buzz when I died;
  The stillness round my form
Was like the stillness in the air
  Between the heaves of storm.

The eyes beside had wrung them dry,
  And breaths were gathering sure
For that last onset, when the king
  Be witnessed in his power.

I willed my keepsakes, signed away
  What portion of me I
Could make assignable,—and then
  There interposed a fly,

With blue, uncertain, stumbling buzz,
  Between the light and me;
And then the windows failed, and then
  I could not see to see.

CXXIX

Adrift! A little boat adrift!
  And night is coming down!
Will no one guide a little boat
  Unto the nearest town?

So sailors say, on yesterday,
Just as the dusk was brown,
One little boat gave up its strife,
And gurgled down and down.

But angels say, on yesterday,
Just as the dawn was red,
One little boat o'erspent with gales
Retrimmed its masts, redecked its sails
Exultant, onward sped!

CXXX

There's been a death in the opposite house
As lately as to-day.
I know it by the numb look
Such houses have always.

The neighbors rustle in and out,
The doctor drives away.
A window opens like a pod,
Abrupt, mechanically;

Somebody flings a mattress out,—
The children hurry by;
They wonder if it died on that,—
I used to when a boy.

The minister goes stiffly in
As if the house were his,
And he owned all the mourners now,
And little boys besides;

And then the milliner, and the man
Of the appalling trade,

To take the measure of the house.
  There'll be that dark parade

Of tassels and of coaches soon;
  It's easy as a sign,—
The intuition of the news
  In just a country town.

CXXXI

We never know we go,—when we are going
  We jest and shut the door;
Fate following behind us bolts it,
  And we accost no more.

CXXXII

It struck me every day
  The lightning was as new
As if the cloud that instant slit
  And let the fire through.

It burned me in the night,
  It blistered in my dream;
It sickened fresh upon my sight
  With every morning's beam.

I thought that storm was brief,—
  The maddest, quickest by;
But Nature lost the date of this,
  And left it in the sky.

CXXXIII

Water is taught by thirst;
Land, by the oceans passed;

Transport, by throe;
Peace, by its battles told;
Love, by memorial mould;
Birds, by the snow.

CXXXIV

We thirst at first,—'t is Nature's act;
And later, when we die,
A little water supplicate
Of fingers going by.

It intimates the finer want,
Whose adequate supply
Is that great water in the west
Termed immortality.

CXXXV

A clock stopped—not the mantel's;
Geneva's farthest skill
Can't put the puppet bowing
That just now dangled still.

An awe came on the trinket!
The figures hunched with pain,
Then quivered out of decimals
Into degreeless noon.

It will not stir for doctors,
This pendulum of snow;
The shopman importunes it,
While cool, concernless No

Nods from the gilded pointers,
Nods from the seconds slim,

Decades of arrogance between
  The dial life and him.

CXXXVI

All overgrown by cunning moss,
  All interspersed with weed,
The little cage of "Currer Bell,"
  In quiet Haworth laid.

This bird, observing others,
  When frosts too sharp became,
Retire to other latitudes,
  Quietly did the same.

But differed in returning;
  Since Yorkshire hills are green,
Yet not in all the nests I meet
  Can nightingale be seen.

Gathered from any wanderings,
  Gethsemane can tell
Through what transporting anguish
  She reached the asphodel!

Soft falls the sounds of Eden
  Upon her puzzled ear;
Oh, what an afternoon for heaven,
  When Brontë entered there!

CXXXVII

A toad can die of light!
Death is the common right
  Of toads and men,—
Of earl and midge

The privilege.
  Why swagger then?
The gnat's supremacy
Is large as thine.

CXXXVIII

Far from love the Heavenly Father
  Leads the chosen child;
Oftener through realm of briar
  Than the meadow mild,

Oftener by the claw of dragon
  Than the hand of friend,
Guides the little one predestined
  To the native land.

CXXXIX

A long, long sleep, a famous sleep
  That makes no show for dawn
By stretch of limb or stir of lid,—
  An independent one.

Was ever idleness like this?
  Within a hut of stone
To bask the centuries away
  Nor once look up for noon?

CXL

'T was just this time last year I died.
  I know I heard the corn,
When I was carried by the farms,—
  It had the tassels on.

I thought how yellow it would look
  When Richard went to mill;
And then I wanted to get out,
  But something held my will.

I thought just how red apples wedged
  The stubble's joints between;
And carts went stooping round the fields
  To take the pumpkins in.

I wondered which would miss me least,
  And when Thanksgiving came,
If father'd multiply the plates
  To make an even sum.

And if my stocking hung too high,
  Would it blur the Christmas glee,
That not a Santa Claus could reach
  The altitude of me?

But this sort grieved myself, and so
  I thought how it would be
When just this time, some perfect year,
  Themselves should come to me.

CXLI

On this wondrous sea,
  Sailing silently,
Knowest thou the shore
  Ho! pilot, ho!
Where no breakers roar,
  Where the storm is o'er?

In the silent west
Many sails at rest,
  Their anchors, fast;
Thither I pilot thee,—
Land, ho! Eternity!
  Ashore at last!

PART FIVE

The Single Hound

One sister have I in our house,
And one a hedge away,
There's only one recorded
But both belong to me.

One came the way that I came
And wore my past year's gown,
The other as a bird her nest,
Builded our hearts among.

She did not sing as we did,
It was a different tune,
Herself to her a music
As Bumble-bee of June.

To-day is far from childhood
But up and down the hills
I held her hand the tighter,
Which shortened all the miles.

And still her hum the years among
Deceives the Butterfly,
Still in her eye the Violets lie
Mouldered this many May.

I spilled the dew but took the morn,
I chose this single star
From out the wide night's numbers,
Sue—forevermore!

EMILY.

I

Adventure most unto itself
The Soul condemned to be;
Attended by a Single Hound—
Its own Identity.

II

The Soul that has a Guest,
Doth seldom go abroad,
Diviner Crowd at home
Obliterate the need,
And courtesy forbid
A Host's departure, when
Upon Himself be visiting
The Emperor of Men!

III

Except the smaller size, no Lives are round,
These hurry to a sphere, and show, and end.
The larger, slower grow, and later hang—
The Summers of Hesperides are long.

IV

Fame is a fickle food
Upon a shifting plate,
Whose table once a Guest, but not
The second time, is set.

Whose crumbs the crows inspect,
And with ironic caw
Flap past it to the Farmer's corn;
Men eat of it and die.

V

The right to perish might be thought
An undisputed right,
Attempt it, and the Universe upon the opposite
Will concentrate its officers—
You cannot even die,
But Nature and Mankind must pause
To pay you scrutiny.

VI

Peril as a possession
'T is good to bear,
Danger disintegrates satiety;
There's Basis there
Begets an awe,
That searches Human Nature's creases
As clean as Fire.

VII

When Etna basks and purrs,
Naples is more afraid
Than when she shows her Garnet Tooth;
Security is loud.

VIII

Reverse cannot befall that fine Prosperity
Whose sources are interior.

As soon Adversity
A diamond overtake,
In far Bolivian ground;
Misfortune hath no implement
Could mar it, if it found.

IX

To be alive is power,
Existence in itself,
Without a further function,
Omnipotence enough.

To be alive and Will—
'T is able as a God!
The Further of ourselves be what—
Such being Finitude?

X

Witchcraft has not a pedigree,
'T is early as our breath,
And mourners meet it going out
The moment of our death.

XI

Exhilaration is the Breeze
That lifts us from the ground,
And leaves us in another place
Whose statement is not found;
Returns us not, but after time
We soberly descend,
A little newer for the term
Upon enchanted ground.

XII

No romance sold unto,
Could so enthrall a man
As the perusal of
His individual one.
'T is fiction's, to dilute
To plausibility
Our novel, when 't is small enough
To credit,—'t isn't true!

XIII

If what we could were what we would—
Criterion be small;
It is the Ultimate of talk
The impotence to tell.

XIV

Perception of an
Object costs
Precise the Object's loss.
Perception in itself a gain
Replying to its price;
The Object Absolute is nought,
Perception sets it fair,
And then upbraids a Perfectness
That situates so far.

XV

No other can reduce
Our mortal consequence,
Like the remembering it be nought
A period from hence.

But contemplation for
Contemporaneous nought
Our single competition;
Jehovah's estimate.

XVI

The blunder is to estimate,—
"Eternity is *Then*,"
We say, as of a station.
Meanwhile he is so near,
He joins me in my ramble,
Divides abode with me,
No friend have I that so persists
As this Eternity.

XVII

My Wheel is in the dark,—
I cannot see a spoke,
Yet know its dripping feet
Go round and round.

My foot is on the tide—
An unfrequented road,
Yet have all roads
A "clearing" at the end.

Some have resigned the Loom,
Some in the busy tomb
Find quaint employ,
Some with new, stately feet
Pass royal through the gate,
Flinging the problem back at you and I.

XVIII

There is another Loneliness
That many die without,
Not want or friend occasions it,
Or circumstances or lot.

But nature sometimes, sometimes thought,
And whoso it befall
Is richer than could be divulged
By mortal numeral.

XIX

So gay a flower bereaved the mind
As if it were a woe,
Is Beauty an affliction, then?
Tradition ought to know.

XX

Glory is that bright tragic thing,
That for an instant
Means Dominion,
Warms some poor name
That never felt the sun,
Gently replacing
In oblivion.

XXI

The missing All prevented me
From missing minor things.
If nothing larger than a World's
Departure from a hinge,

Or Sun's extinction be observed,
'T was not so large that I
Could lift my forehead from my work
For curiosity.

XXII

His mind, of man a secret makes,
I meet him with a start,
He carries a circumference
In which I have no part,
Or even if I deem I do—
He otherwise may know.
Impregnable to inquest,
However neighborly.

XXIII

The suburbs of a secret
A strategist should keep,
Better than on a dream intrude
To scrutinize the sleep.

XXIV

The difference between despair
And fear, is like the one
Between the instant of a wreck,
And when the wreck has been.

The mind is smooth,—no motion—
Contented as the eye
Upon the forehead of a Bust,
That knows it cannot see.

XXV

There is a solitude of space,
A solitude of sea,
A solitude of death, but these
Society shall be,
Compared with that profounder site,
That polar privacy,
A Soul admitted to Itself:
Finite Infinity.

XXVI

The props assist the house
Until the house is built,
And then the props withdraw—
And adequate, erect,
The house supports itself;
Ceasing to recollect
The auger and the carpenter.
Just such a retrospect
Hath the perfected life,
A past of plank and nail,
And slowness,—then the scaffolds drop—
Affirming it a soul.

XXVII

The gleam of an heroic act,
Such strange illumination—
The Possible's slow fuse is lit
By the Imagination!

XXVIII

Of Death the sharpest function,
That, just as we discern,
The Excellence defies us;
Securest gathered then
The fruit perverse to plucking,
But leaning to the sight
With the ecstatic limit
Of unobtained Delight.

XXIX

Down Time's quaint stream
Without an oar,
We are enforced to sail,
Our Port—a secret—
Our Perchance—a gale.
What Skipper would
Incur the risk,
What Buccaneer would ride,
Without a surety from the wind
Or schedule of the tide?

XXX

I bet with every Wind that blew, till Nature in chagrin
Employed a *Fact* to visit me and scuttle my Balloon!

XXXI

The Future never spoke,
Nor will he, like the Dumb,
Reveal by sign or syllable
Of his profound To-come.

But when the news be ripe,
Presents it in the Act—
Forestalling preparation
Escape or substitute.
Indifferent to him
The Dower as the Doom,
His office but to execute
Fate's Telegram to him.

XXXII

Two lengths has every day,
Its absolute extent—
And area superior
By hope or heaven lent.
Eternity will be
Velocity, or pause,
At fundamental signals
From fundamental laws.
To die, is not to go—
On doom's consummate chart
No territory new is staked,
Remain thou as thou art.

XXXIII

The Soul's superior instants
Occur to Her alone,
When friend and earth's occasion
Have infinite withdrawn.

Or she, Herself, ascended
To too remote a height,
For lower recognition
Than Her Omnipotent.

This mortal abolition
Is seldom, but as fair
As Apparition—subject
To autocratic air.

Eternity's disclosure
To favorites, a few,
Of the Colossal substance
Of immortality.

XXXIV

Nature is what we see,
The Hill, the Afternoon—
Squirrel, Eclipse, the Bumble-bee,
Nay—Nature is Heaven.

Nature is what we hear,
The Bobolink, the Sea—
Thunder, the Cricket—
Nay,—Nature is Harmony.

Nature is what we know
But have no art to say,
So impotent our wisdom is
To Her simplicity.

XXXV

Ah, Teneriffe!
Retreating Mountain!
Purples of Ages pause for you,
Sunset reviews her Sapphire Regiment,
Day drops you her red Adieu!

Still, clad in your mail of ices,
Thigh of granite and thew of steel—
Heedless, alike, of pomp or parting,
Ah, Teneriffe!
I'm kneeling still.

XXXVI

She died at play,
Gambolled away
Her lease of spotted hours,
Then sank as gaily as a Turk
Upon a couch of flowers.

Her ghost strolled softly o'er the hill
Yesterday and today,
Her vestments as the silver fleece,
Her countenance as spray.

XXXVII

"Morning" means "Milking" to the Farmer
Dawn to the Apennines—
Dice to the Maid.
"Morning" means just Chance to the Lover—
Just Revelation to the Beloved.
Epicures date a breakfast by it!
Heroes a battle,
The Miller a flood,
Faint-going eyes their lapse
From sighing,
Faith, the Experiment of our Lord!

XXXVIII

A little madness in the Spring
Is wholesome even for the King,
But God be with the Clown,
Who ponders this tremendous scene—
This whole experiment of green,
As if it were his own!

XXXIX

I can't tell you, but you feel it—
Nor can you tell me,
Saints with vanished slate and pencil
Solve our April day.

Sweeter than a vanished Frolic
From a vanished Green!
Swifter than the hoofs of Horsemen
Round a ledge of Dream!

Modest, let us walk among it.
With our "faces veiled,"
As they say polite Archangels
Do, in meeting God.

Not for *me* to prate about it,
Not for *you* to say
To some fashionable Lady—
"Charming April Day!"

Rather Heaven's "Peter Parley,"
By which, Children—slow—
To sublimer recitations
Are prepared to go!

XL

Some Days retired from the rest
In soft distinction lie,
The Day that a companion came—
Or was obliged to die.

XLI

Like Men and Women shadows walk
Upon the hills today,
With here and there a mighty bow,
Or trailing courtesy
To Neighbors, doubtless, of their own;
Not quickened to perceive
Minuter landscape, as Ourselves
And Boroughs where we live.

XLII

The butterfly obtains
But little sympathy,
Though favorably mentioned
In Entomology.
Because he travels freely
And wears a proper coat,
The circumspect are certain
That he is dissolute.
Had he the homely scutcheon of modest Industry,
'T were fitter certifying for Immortality.

XLIII

Beauty crowds me till I die,
Beauty, mercy have on me!

But if I expire today,
Let it be in sight of thee

XLIV

We spy the Forests and the Hills,
The tents to Nature's Show,
Mistake the outside for the in
And mention what we saw.

Could Commentators on the sign
Of Nature's Caravan
Obtain "admission," as a child,
Some Wednesday afternoon?

XLV

I never told the buried gold
Upon the hill that lies,
I saw the sun, his plunder done,
Crouch low to guard his prize.

He stood as near, as stood you here,
A pace had been between—
Did but a snake bisect the brake,
My life had forfeit been.

That was a wondrous booty,
I hope 't was honest gained—
Those were the finest ingots
That ever kissed the spade.

Whether to keep the secret—
Whether to reveal—
Whether, while I ponder
Kidd may sudden sail—

Could a Shrewd advise me
We might e'en divide—
Should a Shrewd betray me—
"Atropos" decide!

XLVI

The largest fire ever known
Occurs each afternoon,
Discovered is without surprise,
Proceeds without concern:
Consumes, and no report to men,
An Occidental town,
Rebuilt another morning
To be again burned down.

XLVII

Bloom upon the Mountain, stated,
Blameless of a name.
Efflorescence of a Sunset—
Reproduced, the same.

Seed, had I, my purple sowing
Should endow the Day,
Not a tropic of the twilight
Show itself away.

Who for tilling, to the Mountain
Come, and disappear—
Whose be Her renown, or fading,
Witness, is not here.

While I state—the solemn petals
Far as North and East,

Far as South and West expanding,
Culminate in rest.

And the Mountain to the Evening
Fit His countenance,
Indicating by no muscle
The Experience.

XLVIII

March is the month of expectation,
The things we do not know,
The Persons of prognostication
Are coming now.
We try to sham becoming firmness,
But pompous joy
Betrays us, as his first betrothal
Betrays a boy.

XLIX

The Duties of the Wind are few—
To cast the Ships at sea,
Establish March,
The Floods escort,
And usher Liberty.

L

The Winds drew off
Like hungry dogs
Defeated of a bone.
Through fissures in
Volcanic cloud
The yellow lightning shown.

The trees held up
Their mangled limbs
Like animals in pain,
When Nature falls
Upon herself,
Beware an Austrian!

LI

I think that the root of the Wind is Water,
It would not sound so deep
Were it a firmamental product,
Airs no Oceans keep—
Mediterranean intonations,
To a Current's ear
There is a maritime conviction
In the atmosphere.

LII

So, from the mould,
Scarlet and gold
Many a Bulb will rise,
Hidden away cunningly
From sagacious eyes.
So, from cocoon
Many a Worm
Leap so Highland gay,
Peasants like me—
Peasants like thee,
Gaze perplexedly.

LIII

The long sigh of the Frog
Upon a Summer's day,

Enacts intoxication
Upon the revery.
But his receding swell
Substantiates a peace,
That makes the ear inordinate
For corporal release.

LIV

A cap of lead across the sky
Was tight and surly drawn,
We could not find the Mighty Face,
The figure was withdrawn.

A chill came up as from a shaft,
Our noon became a well,
A thunderstorm combines the charms
Of Winter and of Hell.

LV

I send two Sunsets—
Day and I in competition ran,
I finished two, and several stars,
While He was making one.

His own is ampler—
But, as I was saying to a friend,
Mine is the more convenient
To carry in the hand.
(Sent with brilliant flowers.)

LVI

Of this is Day composed—
A morning and a noon,

A Revelry unspeakable
And then a gay Unknown;
Whose Pomps allure and spurn—
And dower and deprive,
And penury for glory
Remedilessly leave.

LVII

The Hills erect their purple heads,
The Rivers lean to see—
Yet Man has not, of all the throng,
A curiosity.

LVIII

Lightly stepped a yellow star
To its lofty place,
Loosed the Moon her silver hat
From her lustral face.
All of evening softly lit
As an astral hall—
"Father," I observed to Heaven,
"You are punctual."

LIX

The Moon upon her fluent route
Defiant of a road,
The stars Etruscan argument,
Substantiate a God.
If Aims impel these Astral Ones,
The Ones allowed to know,
Know that which makes them as forgot
As Dawn forgets them now.

LX

Like some old-fashioned miracle
When Summertime is done,
Seems Summer's recollection
And the affairs of June.

As infinite tradition
As Cinderella's bays,
Or little John of Lincoln Green,
Or Bluebeard's galleries.

Her Bees have a fictitious hum,
Her Blossoms, like a dream,
Elate—until we almost weep
So plausible they seem.

Her Memories like strains—review—
When Orchestra is dumb,
The Violin in baize replaced
And Ear and Heaven numb.

LXI

Glowing is her Bonnet,
Glowing is her Cheek,
Glowing is her Kirtle,
Yet she cannot speak!

Better, as the Daisy
From the Summer hill,
Vanish unrecorded
Save by tearful Rill,

Save by loving Sunrise
Looking for her face,

Save by feet unnumbered
Pausing at the place!

LXII

Forever cherished be the tree,
Whose apple Winter warm,
Enticed to breakfast from the sky
Two Gabriels yestermorn;
They registered in Nature's book
As Robin—Sire and Son,
But angels have that modest way
To screen them from renown.

LXIII

The Ones that disappeared are back,
The Phoebe and the Crow,
Precisely as in March is heard
The curtness of the Jay—
Be this an Autumn or a Spring?
My wisdom loses way,
One side of me the nuts are ripe—
The other side is May.

LXIV

Those final Creatures,—who they are—
That, faithful to the close,
Administer her ecstasy,
But just the Summer knows.

LXV

Summer begins to have the look,
Peruser of enchanting Book
Reluctantly, but sure, perceives—
A gain upon the backward leaves.

Autumn begins to be inferred
By millinery of the cloud,
Or deeper color in the shawl
That wraps the everlasting hill.

The eye begins its avarice,
A meditation chastens speech,
Some Dyer of a distant tree
Resumes his gaudy industry.

Conclusion is the course of all,
Almost to be perennial,
And then elude stability
Recalls to immortality.

LXVI

A prompt, executive Bird is the Jay,
Bold as a Bailiff's hymn,
Brittle and brief in quality—
Warrant in every line;

Sitting a bough like a Brigadier,
Confident and straight,
Much is the mien
Of him in March
As a Magistrate.

LXVII

Like brooms of steel
The Snow and Wind
Had swept the Winter Street,
The House was hooked,
The Sun sent out
Faint Deputies of heat—
Where rode the Bird
The Silence tied
His ample, plodding Steed,
The Apple in the cellar snug
Was all the one that played.

LXVIII

These are the days that Reindeer love
And pranks the Northern star,
This is the Sun's objective
And Finland of the year.

LXIX

Follow wise Orion
Till you lose your eye,
Dazzlingly decamping
He is just as high.

LXX

In winter, in my room,
I came upon a worm,
Pink, lank, and warm.
But as he was a worm
And worms presume,
Not quite with him at home—

Secured him by a string
To something neighboring,
And went along.

A trifle afterward
A thing occurred,
I'd not believe it if I heard—
But state with creeping blood;
A snake, with mottles rare,
Surveyed my chamber floor,
In feature as the worm before,
But ringed with power.
The very string
With which I tied him, too,
When he was mean and new,
That string was there.

I shrank—"How fair you are!"
Propitiation's claw—
"Afraid," he hissed,
"Of me?"
"No cordiality?"
He fathomed me.
Then, to a rhythm slim
Secreted in his form,
As patterns swim,
Projected him.

That time I flew,
Both eyes his way,
Lest he pursue—
Nor ever ceased to run,
Till, in a distant town,
Towns on from mine—
I sat me down;
This was a dream.

LXXI

Not any sunny tone
From any fervent zone
Finds entrance there.
Better a grave of Balm
Toward human nature's home,
And Robins near,
Than a stupendous Tomb
Proclaiming to the gloom
How dead we are.

LXXII

For Death,—or rather
For the things 't will buy,
These put away
Life's opportunity.

The things that Death will buy
Are Room,—Escape
From Circumstances,
And a Name.
How gifts of Life
With Death's gifts will compare,
We know not—
For the rates stop Here.

LXXIII

Dropped into the
Ether Acre!
Wearing the sod gown—
Bonnet of Everlasting laces—
Brooch frozen on!
Horses of blonde—

And coach of silver,
Baggage a strapped Pearl!
Journey of Down
And whip of Diamond—
Riding to meet the Earl!

LXXIV

This quiet Dust was Gentlemen and Ladies,
  And Lads and Girls;
Was laughter and ability and sighing,
  And frocks and curls.

This passive place a Summer's nimble mansion,
  Where Bloom and Bees
Fulfilled their Oriental Circuit,
  Then ceased like these.

LXXV

'T was comfort in her dying room
To hear the living clock,
A short relief to have the wind
Walk boldly up and knock,
Diversion from the dying theme
To hear the children play,
But wrong, the mere
That these could live,—
And This of ours must die!

LXXVI

Too cold is this
To warm with sun,
Too stiff to bended be,
To joint this agate were a feat

Outstaring masonry.
How went the agile kernel out—
Contusion of the husk,
Nor rip, nor wrinkle indicate,—
But just an Asterisk.

LXXVII

I watched her face to see which way
She took the awful news,
Whether she died before she heard—
Or in protracted bruise
Remained a few short years with us,
Each heavier than the last—
A further afternoon to fail,
As Flower at fall of Frost.

LXXVIII

To-day or this noon
She dwelt so close,
I almost touched her;
Tonight she lies
Past neighborhood—
And bough and steeple—
Now past surmise.

LXXIX

I see thee better in the dark,
I do not need a light.
The love of thee a prism be
Excelling violet.

I see thee better for the years
That hunch themselves between,

The miner's lamp sufficient be
To nullify the mine.

And in the grave I see thee best—
Its little panels be
A-glow, all ruddy with the light
I held so high for thee!

What need of day to those whose dark
Hath so surpassing sun,
It seem it be continually
At the meridian?

LXXX

Low at my problem bending,
Another problem comes,
Larger than mine, serener,
Involving statelier sums;
I check my busy pencil,
My ciphers slip away,
Wherefore, my baffled fingers,
Time Eternity?

LXXXI

If pain for peace prepares,
Lo the "Augustan" years
Our feet await!

If Springs from Winter rise,
Can the Anemone's
Be reckoned up?

If night stands first, then noon,
To gird us for the sun,
What gaze—

When, from a thousand skies,
On our developed eyes
Noons blaze!

LXXXII

I fit for them,
I seek the dark till I am thorough fit.
The labor is a solemn one,
With this sufficient sweet—
That abstinence as mine produce
A purer good for them,
If I succeed,—
If not, I had
The transport of the Aim.

LXXXIII

Not one by Heaven defrauded stay,
Although He seem to steal,
He restitutes in some sweet way.
Secreted in His will.

LXXXIV

The feet of people walking home
In gayer sandals go,
The Crocus, till she rises,
The Vassal of the Snow—
The lips at Hallelujah!
Long years of practice bore,
Till bye and bye these Bargemen
Walked singing on the shore.

Pearls are the Diver's farthings
Extorted from the Sea,

Pinions the Seraph's wagon,
Pedestrians once, as we—
Night is the morning's canvas,
Larceny, legacy,
Death but our rapt attention
To immortality.

My figures fail to tell me
How far the village lies,
Whose Peasants are the angels,
Whose Cantons dot the skies,
My Classics veil their faces,
My Faith that dark adores,
Which from its solemn Abbeys
Such resurrection pours!

LXXXV

We should not mind so small a flower,
Except it quiet bring
Our little garden that we lost
Back to the lawn again.
So spicy her Carnations red,
So drunken reel her Bees,
So silver steal a hundred Flutes
From out a hundred trees,
That whoso sees this little flower,
By faith may clear behold
The Bobolinks around the throne,
And Dandelions gold.

LXXXVI

To the staunch Dust we safe commit thee;
Tongue if it hath, inviolate to thee—

Silence denote and Sanctity enforce thee,
Passenger of Infinity!

LXXXVII

Her "Last Poems"—
Poets ended,
Silver perished with her tongue,
Not on record bubbled other
Flute, or Woman, so divine;
Not unto its Summer morning
Robin uttered half the tune—
Gushed too free for the adoring,
From the Anglo-Florentine.
Late the praise—
'T is dull conferring
On a Head too high to crown,
Diadem or Ducal showing,
Be its Grave sufficient sign.
Yet if we, no Poet's kinsman,
Suffocate with easy woe,
What and if ourself a Bridegroom,
Put Her down, in Italy?

LXXXVIII

Immured in Heaven! What a Cell!
Let every bondage be,
Thou Sweetest of the Universe,
Like that which ravished thee!

LXXXIX

I'm thinking of that other morn,
When Cerements let go,

And Creatures clad in Victory
Go up in two by two!

XC

The overtakelessness of those
Who have accomplished Death,
Majestic is to me beyond
The majesties of Earth.
The soul her "not at Home"
Inscribes upon the flesh,
And takes her fair aerial gait
Beyond the hope of touch.

XCI

The Look of Thee, what is it like?
Hast thou a hand or foot,
Or mansion of Identity,
And what is thy Pursuit?

Thy fellows,—are they Realms or Themes?
Hast thou Delight or Fear
Or Longing,—and is that for us
Or values more severe?

Let change transfuse all other traits,
Enact all other blame,
But deign this least certificate—
That thou shalt be the same.

XCII

The Devil, had he fidelity,
Would be the finest friend—

Because he has ability,
But Devils cannot mend.
Perfidy is the virtue
That would he but resign,—
The Devil, so amended,
Were durably divine.

XCIII

Papa above!
                    Regard a Mouse
O'erpowered by the Cat;
Reserve within thy Kingdom
A "mansion" for the Rat!

Snug in seraphic cupboards
To nibble all the day,
While unsuspecting cycles
Wheel pompously away.

XCIV

Not when we know
The Power accosts,
The garment of Surprise
Was all our timid Mother wore
At Home, in Paradise.

XCV

Elijah's wagon knew no thill,
Was innocent of wheel,
Elijah's horses as unique
As was his vehicle.
Elijah's journey to portray,
Expire with him the skill,

Who justified Elijah,
In feats inscrutable.

XCVI

"Remember me," implored the Thief—
Oh magnanimity!
"My Visitor in Paradise
I give thee Guaranty."

That courtesy will fair remain,
When the delight is dust,
With which we cite this mightiest case
Of compensated Trust.

Of All, we are allowed to hope,
But Affidavit stands
That this was due, where some, we fear,
Are unexpected friends.

XCVII

To this apartment deep
No ribaldry may creep;
Untroubled this abode
By any man but God.

XCVIII

"Sown in dishonor?"
Ah! Indeed!
May this dishonor be?
If I were half so fine myself,
I'd notice nobody!
"Sown in corruption?"
By no means!

Apostle is askew;
Corinthians 1:15, narrates
A circumstance or two!

XCIX

Through lane it lay, through bramble,
Through clearing and through wood,
Banditti often passed us
Upon the lonely road.

The wolf came purring curious,
The owl looked puzzled down,
The serpent's satin figure
Glid stealthily along.

The tempest touched our garments,
The lightning's poignards gleamed,
Fierce from the crag above us
The hungry vulture screamed.

The satyr's fingers beckoned,
The valley murmured "Come"—
These were the mates—and this the road
Those children fluttered home.

C

Who is it seeks my pillow nights?
With plain inspecting face,
"Did you, or did you not?" to ask,
'T is Conscience, childhood's nurse.

With martial hand she strokes the hair
Upon my wincing head,
"All rogues shall have their part in"—

What—
The Phosphorus of God.

CI

His Cheek is his Biographer—
As long as he can blush,
Perdition is Opprobrium;
Past that, he sins in peace.
Thief

CII

"Heavenly Father," take to thee
The supreme iniquity,
Fashioned by thy candid hand
In a moment contraband.
Though to trust us seem to us
More respectful—"we are dust."
We apologize to Thee
For Thine own Duplicity.

CIII

The sweets of Pillage can be known
To no one but the Thief,
Compassion for Integrity
Is his divinest Grief.

CIV

The Bible is an antique volume
Written by faded men,
At the suggestion of Holy Spectres—
Subjects—Bethlehem—
Eden—the ancient Homestead—

Satan—the Brigadier,
Judas—the great Defaulter,
David—the Troubadour.
Sin—a distinguished Precipice
Others must resist,
Boys that "believe"
Are very lonesome—
Other boys are "lost."
Had but the tale a warbling Teller
All the boys would come—
Orpheus's sermon captivated,
It did not condemn.

CV

A little over Jordan,
As Genesis record,
An Angel and a Wrestler
Did wrestle long and hard.

Till, morning touching mountain,
And Jacob waxing strong,
The Angel begged permission
To breakfast and return.

"Not so," quoth wily Jacob,
And girt his loins anew,
"Until thou bless me, stranger!"
The which acceded to:

Light swung the silver fleeces
Peniel hills among,
And the astonished Wrestler
Found he had worsted God!

CVI

Dust is the only secret,
Death the only one
You cannot find out all about
In his native town:
Nobody knew his father,
Never was a boy,
Hadn't any playmates
Or early history.
Industrious, laconic,
Punctual, sedate,
Bolder than a Brigand,
Swifter than a Fleet,
Builds like a bird too,
Christ robs the nest—
Robin after robin
Smuggled to rest!

CVII

Ambition cannot find him,
Affection doesn't know
How many leagues of Nowhere
Lie between them now.
Yesterday undistinguished—
Eminent to-day,
For our mutual honor—
Immortality!

CVIII

Eden is that old-fashioned House
We dwell in every day,
Without suspecting our abode
Until we drive away.

How fair, on looking back, the Day
We sauntered from the door,
Unconscious our returning
Discover it no more.

CIX

Candor, my tepid Friend,
Come not to play with me!
The Myrrhs and Mochas of the Mind
Are its Iniquity.

CX

Speech is a symptom of affection,
And Silence one,
The perfectest communication
Is heard of none—
Exists and its endorsement
Is had within—
Behold! said the Apostle,
Yet had not seen.

CXI

Who were "the Father and the Son"—
We pondered when a child,
And what had they to do with us—
And when portentous told
With inference appalling,
By Childhood fortified,
We thought, "at least they are no worse
Than they have been described."

Who are "the Father and the Son"—
Did we demand today,

"The Father and the Son" himself
Would doubtless specify,
But had they the felicity
When we desired to know,
We better Friends had been, perhaps,
Than time ensue to be.

We start, to learn that we believe
But once, entirely—
Belief, it does not fit so well
When altered frequently.
We blush, that Heaven if we achieve,
Event ineffable—
We shall have shunned, until ashamed
To own the Miracle.

CXII

That Love is all there is,
Is all we know of Love;
It is enough, the freight should be
Proportioned to the groove.

CXIII

The luxury to apprehend
The luxury 't would be
To look at thee a single time,
An Epicure of me,
In whatsoever Presence, makes,
Till, for a further food
I scarcely recollect to starve,
So first am I supplied.
The luxury to meditate
The luxury it was

To banquet on thy Countenance,
A sumptuousness bestows
On plainer days,
Whose table, far as
Certainty can see,
Is laden with a single crumb—
The consciousness of Thee.

CXIV

The Sea said "Come" to the Brook,
The Brook said "Let me grow!"
The Sea said "Then you will be a Sea—
I want a brook, Come now!"

CXV

All I may, if small,
Do it not display
Larger for its Totalness?
'T is economy
To bestow a world
And withhold a star,
Utmost is munificence;
Less, though larger, Poor.

CXVI

Love reckons by itself alone,
"As large as I" relate the Sun
To one who never felt it blaze,
Itself is all the like it has.

CXVII

The inundation of the Spring
Submerges every soul,
It sweeps the tenement away
But leaves the water whole.
In which the Soul, at first alarmed,
Seeks furtive for its shore,
But acclimated, gropes no more
For that Peninsular.

CXVIII

No Autumn's intercepting chill
Appalls this Tropic Breast,
But African exuberance
And Asiatic Rest.

CXIX

Volcanoes be in Sicily
And South America,
I judge from my geography.
Volcanoes nearer here,

A lava step, at any time,
Am I inclined to climb,
A crater I may contemplate,
Vesuvius at home.

CXX

Distance is not the realm of Fox,
Nor by relay as Bird;
Abated, Distance is until
Thyself, Beloved!

CXXI

The treason of an accent
Might vilify the Joy—
To breathe,—corrode the rapture
Of Sanctity to be.

CXXII

How destitute is he
Whose Gold is firm,
Who finds it every time,
The small stale sum—
When Love, with but a pence
Will so display,
As is a disrespect to India!

CXXIII

Crisis is sweet and, set of Heart
Upon the hither side,
Has dowers of prospective
Surrendered by the Tried.
Inquire of the closing Rose
Which Rapture she preferred,
And she will tell you, sighing,
The transport of the Bud.

CXXIV

To tell the beauty would decrease,
To state the Spell demean,
There is a syllableless sea
Of which it is the sign.

My will endeavours for its word
And fails, but entertains
A rapture as of legacies—
Of introspective mines.

CXXV

To love thee, year by year,
May less appear
Than sacrifice and cease.
However, Dear,

Forever might be short
I thought, to show,
And so I pieced it with a flower now.

CXXVI

I showed her heights she never saw—
"Wouldst climb?" I said,
She said "Not so"—
"With me?" I said, "With me?"
I showed her secrets
Morning's nest,
The rope that Nights were put across—
And *now*, "Wouldst have me for a Guest?"
She could not find her yes—
And then, I brake my life, and Lo!
A light for her, did solemn glow,
The larger, as her face withdrew—
And could she, further, "No?"

CXXVII

On my volcano grows the grass,—
A meditative spot,

An area for a bird to choose
Would be the general thought.

How red the fire reeks below,
How insecure the sod—
Did I disclose, would populate
With awe my solitude.

CXXVIII

If I could tell how glad I was,
I should not be so glad,
But when I cannot make the Force
Nor mould it into word,
I know it is a sign
That new Dilemma be
From mathematics further off,
Than from Eternity.

CXXIX

Her Grace is all she has,
And that, so vast displays,
One Art, to recognize, must be,
Another Art to praise.

CXXX

No matter where the Saints abide,
They make their circuit fair;
Behold how great a Firmament
Accompanies a star!

CXXXI

To see her is a picture,
To hear her is a tune,
To know her an intemperance
As innocent as June;

By which to be undone
Is dearer than Redemption—
Which never to receive,
Makes mockery of melody
It might have been to live.

CXXXII

So set its sun in thee,
What day is dark to me—
What distance far,
So I the ships may see
That touch how seldomly
Thy shore?

CXXXIII

Had this one day not been,
Or could it cease to be—
How smitten, how superfluous
Were every other day!

Lest Love should value less
What Loss would value more,
Had it the stricken privilege—
It cherishes before.

CXXXIV

That she forgot me was the least,
I felt it second pain,
That I was worthy to forget
What most I thought upon.

Faithful, was all that I could boast,
But Constancy became,
To her, by her innominate,
A something like a shame.

CXXXV

The incidents of Love
Are more than its Events,
Investments best expositor
Is the minute per cents.

CXXXVI

A little overflowing word
That any hearing had inferred
For ardor or for tears,
Though generations pass away,
Traditions ripen and decay,
As eloquent appears.

CXXXVII

Just so, Jesus raps—He does not weary—
Last at the knocker and first at the bell,
Then on divinest tiptoe standing
Might He out-spy the lady's soul.
When He retires, chilled and weary—
It will be ample time for me;

Patient, upon the steps, until then—
Heart, I am knocking low at Thee!

CXXXVIII

Safe Despair it is that raves,
Agony is frugal,
Puts itself severe away
For its own perusal.

Garrisoned no Soul can be
In the front of Trouble,
Love is one, not aggregate,
Nor is Dying double.

CXXXIX

The Face we choose to miss,
Be it but for a day—
As absent as a hundred years
When it has rode away.

CXL

Of so divine a loss
We enter but the gain,
Indemnity for loneliness
That such a bliss has been.

CXLI

The healed Heart shows its shallow scar
With confidential moan,
Not mended by Mortality
Are fabrics truly torn.

To go its convalescent way
So shameless is to see,
More genuine were Perfidy
Than such Fidelity.

CXLII

Give little anguish
Lives will fret.
Give avalanches—
And they'll slant,
Straighten, look cautious for their breath,
But make no syllable—
Like Death,
  Who only shows his
  Marble disc—
Sublimer sort than speech.

CXLIII

To pile like Thunder to its close,
Then crumble grand away,
While everything created hid—
This would be Poetry:
Or Love,—the two coeval came—
We both and neither prove,
Experience either, and consume—
For none see God and live.

CXLIV

The Stars are old, that stood for me—
The West a little worn,
Yet newer glows the only Gold
I ever cared to earn—
Presuming on that lone result

Her infinite disdain,
But vanquished her with my defeat,
'T was Victory was slain.

CXLV

All circumstances are the frame
In which His Face is set,
All Latitudes exist for His
Sufficient continent.

The light His Action and the dark
The Leisure of His Will,
In Him Existence serve, or set
A force illegible.

CXLVI

I did not reach thee,
But my feet slip nearer every day;
Three Rivers and a Hill to cross,
One Desert and a Sea—
I shall not count the journey one
When I am telling thee.

Two deserts—but the year is cold
So that will help the sand—
One desert crossed, the second one
Will feel as cool as land.
Sahara is too little price
To pay for thy Right hand!

The sea comes last. Step merry, feet!
So short have we to go
To play together we are prone,
But we must labor now,

The last shall be the lightest load
That we have had to draw.

The Sun goes crooked—that is night—
Before he makes the bend
We must have passed the middle sea,
Almost we wish the end
Were further off—too great it seems
So near the Whole to stand.

We step like plush, we stand like snow—
The waters murmur now,
Three rivers and the hill are passed,
Two deserts and the sea!
Now Death usurps my premium
And gets the look at Thee.

INDEX OF FIRST LINES

E

F

I

J

L

M

N

O

P

R

T

Y